# SPACE TIGER

# SPACE TIGER

## (BOOK 1)

### S.R. SHUJA

First Edition

Cover page: S R Shuja & Saqib Chowdhury

Printed in the United States of America

Publisher:  Mind Talkers Publishing
Ajax, Ontario, Canada

ISBN #:978-0-9878187-8-2

Visit www.mindtalkers.com

To the future Earthling Martians

# Chapter 1

Anybody who had seen Taz in school wouldn't even believe what he did during his free time. He was fourteen, medium height, with a head full of untidy brownish hair. His mother was not somebody who took any kind of untidiness very easily, but Taz had little time to worry about that. One might wonder what was that he was so busy with. He was exceptionally quiet in the class, making it a point not to open his mouth unless any teacher specifically showed deep interest in having him and only him answering any particular question. Perhaps bothered with such events, sometimes he even showed clear reluctance to attend school, which, of course, never materialized.

After school he spent majority of his time in his room. Fearing some sort of anti social tendency his parents made it a burden upon them to call him for everything that they felt might interest him. They were not particularly worried about Taz, a smart and intelligent teenager, who happened to be on the quieter side among their three sons. Under normal circumstances they allowed him to be in his own world.

**April, 2111. May 5. Tuesday**

Returning from school Taz locked himself in his room and checked around carefully. It was important for him to ensure that his secret world remained hidden from the rest of the family. Not noticing anything suspicious, he turned on his GHR (global holographic receiver). The ever smiling face of the CI – 6 (Controller of Investigators # 6) popped up right before him. This particular technology had progressed very much in the recent years. The images often looked so real that one could even forget that it was really a virtual conversation.

"So, how are things my dear junior investigator Mr. Taz?" CI-6 spoke in a humanly voice.

"Good, CI-6," Taz spoke very quietly. He had very little trust in his two younger brothers. At the age of ten and eight everything in the world, no matter how insignificant, was matter of utmost mystery to them. Especially they were morbidly pulled into anything that even remotely had anything to do with Taz.

"You must have received my message," CI-6 tried its best to make the smiling face a tiny bit serious. Taz knew that Bureau of Space Detectives had several of these machines called *controllers*, who managed all space detectives, both junior and senior, and spaceships.

"I did. That's why I called you up as soon as I got back from school," Taz eagerly said.

Connectivity had advanced greatly in recent years. Nowadays tiny devices called Telepathic device (briefly TD) could be implanted into brain. Using these devices it was possible to communicate through thoughts, giving an impression of being telepathic. Many long term studies were being conducted for years to determine the impact of such devices on human brain and mind. Nothing had been found to suggest any harmful effect, yet most people did not feel comfortable implanting such devices inside their brains. Taz's parents were incredibly weary of such technologies. Proven or not, they had made a point to keep any such intrusive technology out of their family. Taz received his from BSD, without the consent of his parents. This might sound odd but BSD had constitutional right to do so provided the detective was fourteen years or older and had consented. However, bureau advised younger users to use the device only for receiving messages when possible. For two way communication he usually used his GHR. CI-6 frequently sent messages to his TD. There were many varieties of the device. The one he received from the bureau was called *Mind Reader*.

"What are you going to do if you get a chance to go to Mars?" CI-6 asked, grinning.

"Mars! Really? Did anything happen there?" Taz tried to control his excitement. He was asking to be sent to Mars for a while, but had no luck. As a junior investigator, he was limited to earth's orbit to gain more experience. While such expeditions were not particularly devoid of excitement, his eyes were far beyond in the space. Noticing his ever increasing enthusiasm, he was promised to receive a consideration when the next opportunity came. This sounded much better than it really was. There were hundreds of novice to skilled detectives waited in the Mars queue and winning a place was no easier than winning a lottery. Was it finally happening?

"Yes, something horrible has happened," CI-6 grimly said. "We have decided to send a team there. The Captain Detective of the spaceship has asked for a young team. Your name came up above all the potential candidates for trainees. If you want to go, I can arrange for you to be included."

Taz burst into excitement. "I definitely want to go. Which team?"

"Space Tiger."

"Space Tiger!" Taz pumped his fists in the air in sheer joy. Space Tiger was the spaceship lead by Captain Detective Pete. He was young in age but had proven himself to be one of the top detectives. Many experienced senior detectives lined up to get an opportunity to fly with him. Just in a few years Pete had become a legend in the department. Taz had read and heard so much about him that sometimes he had difficulty believing that Pete was only 22.

"Doesn't look like you are interested," CI-6 joked. His ever smiling face turned even brighter attempting to simulate human emotion.

"No, no, I want to go," Taz insisted.

"Ha…ha…ha…I know, I know. You don't need to tell me that," CI-6 simulated laughter. "However, there is still one question that needs to be answered – will your parents permit you? For you to go to Mars, you need their approval. That's a rule for long distance travel for underage detectives. As you already know, going up just to the earth's orbit does not require it."

Taz's heart sunk. He had not yet disclosed his attachment to BSD to his parents. It was Uncle Alam, his father's youngest brother, who had made it possible for him to join BSD. Uncle Alam was a reputed pilot who flew very fast fighter planes. Most thought he would eventually join the space detectives. But his wife had been totally against it. As a result he had to stay away from BSD. Once retired from his job as a fighter plane pilot, he had taken it upon him to find talented young men and women to be recruited in BSD. Knowing how much Taz loved flying, he had heavily encouraged him to consider joining BSD. He was basically the one who had taught Taz a lot of things about flying. When Taz started to show some serious skill, he sent him to sit in the initial series of tests for space detectives. No parental permission was required. Both of his parents shared such fear of height that asking for their permission would simply mean burying it all.

Not just the initial tests, Taz aced all the tests to stun everybody. Two years had passed since then. His training had continued without the consent of his parents. He was also sent to the earth's orbit several times. Uncle Alam had signed as his guardian. Being a kin, his consent was considered good enough for such training activities.

Many companies, big or small, had been crowding the Earth's orbit with their own manned space stations as commercial entities for some time now. Some of them had people living there year around. Some others accepted regular tourists for a hefty fee. Even though no organized criminal groups had been able to gain a strong footing there, crimes did get committed. One such notable event had happened several years ago when a scientist killed two of his assistant researchers. Later he was found to be mentally unwell. Usually petty thefts to skirmishes were most frequent events. But sometimes big things happened too; things that required some serious attention.

Some time in the past, many countries in the world had coordinated and signed an agreement to keep all matters in the space to keep out of the reach of earthly politics. Bad things still happened. Some powerful countries tried planting spy equipments secretively. After several such cases were unearthed accidentally, the need for an organization investigating such occurrences became necessary. U.S.A. first proposed it and several wealthy and powerful countries agreed. That was when BSD (Bureau of Space Detectives) was born. In the beginning space detectives were primarily assigned to investigate espionage cases. However, over the years their responsibility had grown and they were eventually expected to work as the extension of police in space, and frequently took up cases for various crimes. Taz hadn't yet been involved in any complex cases. Only the best and experienced were allowed to investigate those. He had been waiting for what seemed to him eternity for a case like that.

Uncle Alam had immense confidence in Taz. He believed that Taz would progress in a phenomenal speed. Bureau of Space Detectives had accepted him as a trainee based on the analysis of all the tests he sat for, where he showed excellent observational skill along with exceptional ability to learn new things. Later he had easily established himself as a talented individual, who could learn to fly new machines relatively faster than other trainees of his age. He had wowed with his high scores during simulated flying. There was also another particular reason why he was quickly becoming a favorite among the instructors – he could remain calm and effective even in challenging situations. His problem solving abilities were yet to be proven, but he was determined and ambitious, and hoped to make a great space detective some day.

"That is not a good thing," Taz thoughtfully said. "I need to discuss this with Uncle Alam; hopefully he'll find a way out. When is the departure? What is the duration? Who are the team members?"

"Duration is estimated to be four five days," CI-6 said, "May be longer. Depends on how things go there. There will be five crews in the team beside Pete. None of the crews has been finalized yet. Pete received a list of all potential crews. He is in the process of making his selections. I need your parent's approval by tomorrow. Once I have it, I'll finalize your membership."

Taz shrugged. He knew this day was coming. He had little choice but to rely on Uncle Alam. Whatever happened, just being selected by Pete was by itself a great achievement for a young space detective.

"Does Pete know me?" He asked.

"He knows you by name. I provided all the details. He was quick to select you. That's a very good thing. Now, son, go get your parents blessing. I must leave now. Bye, bye." He disconnected.

Taz thought it out for a little while before reaching

for the phone. Uncle Alam did not like holography or telepathy. There were only two ways to contact him – by phone or in person.

# Chapter 2

Daniel Martin, known briefly as Dan, observed Taz keenly for a long time, at least that's how it seemed. He was taller than average, twice as wide as he should have been, had a short beard and a shiny bald head. He wore a large pair of glasses. All together he looked quite the weird. But Taz liked him the first time he met him. Even though he almost never smiled, it didn't take too long to figure out that deep inside he was an easy going, friendly gentleman. He was the chief of BSD. For Taz to make the trip to Mars, his approval was a must.

"Listen son, I had to suffer quite a bit because of you." He looked grave serious. "I must admit, I have never before met any parents as concerned as yours. They overwhelmed me with their incessant questions. I definitely don't appreciate the fact that you haven't told them anything about BSD. That uncle of yours...Alam...is gonna get it someday from me..." Dan made a gesture as if he was about to slap somebody's buttocks. Taz laughed out loud. He probably shouldn't have, but he couldn't help it.

"So you found it very funny? Good, good. I like happy kids. Have you met Pete yet?"

"Not yet." Since coming to New York Taz had been

looking for an opportunity to meet Pete, but had no luck yet.

"Your flight is still four to five hours away. He'll show up before that. Have you met the other crews?"

Taz shook his head. "No."

Since Taz had the after school meeting with CI-6, things had moved quite fast. So much had happened in just couple of days that he felt sort of dazed!

First of all, he and Uncle Alam had to sit with his parents for a long discussion. His parents initially were very elated hearing about his excellence in flying; however, as soon as they heard about the Mars trip they went for an abrupt U turn. *He was only a little boy. How could he go that far all by himself? How about his studies? Who was going to look after him?* Etc. Etc. Uncle Alam tried his best to calm them down. *There was no need to worry about his studies. He could do his homework sitting right inside the spaceship. If school permitted he could even attend school remotely.*

School had no objection whatsoever. The principal and the teaching staff were very proud knowing that one of their students was going to Mars as a member of elite BSD. Even that wasn't enough for his parents. They called up Dan and arranged for a personal meeting. The half an hour meeting stretched to two hours. Then they had Dan sign a ten page long contract with numerous conditions. Dan also had to give them personal assurance that he would send Taz only with the captain who was the best of the best. He even provided them with a brief biography of Pete. While they were impressed with his skill and achievement as a space detective, they were quite worried with the fact that he himself was *so young*!

Anyway, at the end they approved. Taz couldn't be happier. Not only he was going to Mars, he was going there to investigate an important case. He didn't have all the details yet, but that didn't matter. He was the youngest ever to get such an opportunity.

Even though he hadn't meet Pete yet, he had seen him in pictures. Pete appeared to have a ruggedly handsome face with a pair of soft eyes and a mysterious smile. He had a reputation as a friendly, down to earth young man. Taz wondered how good Pete had to be to become the Captain Detective of a large spaceship like Space Tiger at his age. Many senior detectives could only dream about it.

The Space Tiger was scheduled to start at midnight from the Space station in New York. Taz had never visited the NY Space station before. Around 10 PM Dan arrived at the Space station with him from his BSD office in Manhattan. The organization had provided him a flying car for his convenience. Even though for years many companies in America, Europe and Asia had the technology to build very efficient flying cars, that could both drive on the road and fly, governments around the world were yet to allow massive production of them. They were weary of the fact that once allowed in the market, controlling the flying traffic would become a nightmare. Number of accidents would skyrocket, death tolls jump. Hence, only a handful of people were permitted to have them and that was also after going through immense trouble to justify.

Hours passed by. Pete hadn't shown up. Clearly Dan was feeling a little impatient. His calls were not being answered. Where could Pete be? He called up CI-6, who informed him that Pete was in the middle of a thorough checking of his spaceship. This was customary for every captain. For Pete it was like religion. When done he would come and get Taz, they were told.

Dan shrugged in despair. "He doesn't trust anybody. This spaceship is not departing at midnight. He isn't going to take off until he finds everything to his complete satisfaction. Don't get me wrong. It's good to be cautious. But we have the best technicians in the world. Let's not forget that."

Taz sat calmly, trying to hide his excitement. His flight from Dhaka to New York took only three hours. It had been a while since special space flights became part of regular long distance flying within the earth bound destinations. These fast flying airplanes flew much higher than regular planes, reducing the travel time extensively. It was Taz's first trip in such flights. The tickets were pricy. This time BSD picked up the tab.

Sitting quietly, Taz must have dozed off for a moment or so. A gentle touch on his shoulder startled him into reality. A young, red-haired girl stood before him. She smiled. "Come with me."

Dan wasn't around. He must have gone to check something. Taz hesitated for a moment. He didn't know this girl. She smiled again. "Dan went to see Pete. He didn't want to wake you up. You travelled half the world. Jet lag. Don't worry. Come with me. We are almost ready for departure."

"Who are you?" Taz asked, still not sure.

"Oh, I totally forgot to introduce myself," the girl said shyly. "I am Larisa. I am a trainee from Brazil." She shook hands. "I know everything about you. You are good at flying. Come on. We are getting late."

They walked past several corridors with highly secured doors and even a few armed guards before entering a specious lobby with shiny marble floor. Several dozens of uniformed employees could be seen busily moving around. Every door to this lobby was guarded by armed men. This part of the Space station was out of reach for general public. They found Pete and Dan standing at one corner and discussing something on a rather serious posture. Instead of approaching them, Larisa led him to another corridor and climbed into a waiting tram.

"Where are we going?" asked Taz as the tram slowly moved ahead.

"To the spaceship," Larisa smiled. "This must be your first time in Space Tiger."

Taz nodded. He had been to several spaceships, but not to anything that was capable of travelling as far as Mars or beyond. The tram stopped inside a huge metallic dome after a short trip. As he stepped out of it, what captured his view left him in awe. The Space Tiger! It must have been more than two hundred feet long, over forty feet in height. Two half circled wings were placed back to back on a hundred feet long cylindrical base, giving an impression of a leaping tiger. Each of the wings was at least a hundred feet in diameter. At the front section of the cylindrical base rested a saucer module on a strong and sturdy pillar. With a diameter of fifty feet, the saucer was three storied high, consisted of the cockpit, all the control mechanisms and sleeping cabins for the crew. All together, a stunningly beautiful craft.

"Pretty, huh?" Larisa said, dreamily.

"Absolutely! Have you travelled in it before?"

"Nope. This is going to be my first too. But I have been inside the ship before. I came with my flying school. Let's go in. We'll go to the cockpit first. All the crews are there."

Taz followed Larisa down the stairs to a platform almost fifty feet below ground level. Two security guards stopped them here and put them through scanners and checked their ID cards. Past checkpoint they hopped onto an escalator that brought them up to the broad entrance of the saucer. The heavy gate opened and closed silently as they stepped inside into a narrow corridor. Ten steps ahead they found another door that led them into the specious cockpit.

Since joining BSD Taz had the opportunity to ride and fly several spaceships. While each of them was somewhat different in size and shape, they all had specious cockpits. Keeping to that trend, Space Tiger had even larger cockpit that was round and at least 40 feet in diameter. At the front the entire wall was mostly covered with panels with all kind of levers, buttons and monitors. There were several cushioned seats in front of these panels for the crews to sit. On the back near the walls were placed several tables and chairs all stuck to the floor. The floor was completely covered by a thick special type of carpet called *gravity carpet*. This was a standard addition to almost all the spaceships. The goal was to reduce or eliminate any negative impact on the space travelers due to the lack of gravity. The carpet was used along with specially made space suits to provide a sense of gravity. The popular concept of gravity wheel had been around for a while, but there was still no true gravity wheel built. One of the major issues was just to create same amount of gravitational force as on earth, the wheel had to spin around its axis two times a minute. But people would get sick inside an object that was spinning that fast unless it was at least seven hundred feet in diameter. The amount of money that would require building such a large ship was hard to come. As a result, all kind of alternatives popped up.

There was another automatic door behind the tables. Taz assumed the crew cabins were behind that door. The cockpit was empty. Taz was a little surprised. He was hoping to find the other crews here.

"They must be getting ready," Larisa said. "Let me show you your cabin. All the cabins are on the lower level. We have to put on our suits too."

Taz followed Larisa through the second door into a small elevator lobby. The elevator sensed their presence and the door opened up. Larisa walked inside signaling him to do the same. The elevator was quick and they were on the floor below in seconds. There were total eight cabins on both sides of a short passage. Six of them had name plates. He was happy seeing one of them was his. "This must be my cabin," he said.

Larisa nodded. "Yes. Separate cabins for each. Pete takes privacy very seriously. Most spaceships are space constrained. You have been into many, so you must know."

She slowly pushed the door of the cabin to open it wide. The cabin was no less than twelve feet by twelve feet. No windows. Like in most spaceships, the bed and the mattress were nicely hidden inside the wall.   A button could be pressed to have them popped out silently. The table, chairs and other furniture were all made keeping in mind that they didn't take any more space than absolutely needed. There was a large monitor on one of the walls. Clearly, this was the only means to see outside view.

When a small button on the wall was pressed a portion of the wall quietly moved to reveal a small closet. There were several unusual looking suits inside it. "Nano powered," said Larisa.

"Isn't there a gravity wheel in this ship?" Taz asked, little surprised. These suits were used to cope up with lack of gravity. As far as he knew, Space Tiger had a gravity wheel though not a full sized one. He had read about it. The half circled wings could be turned to join together to create a round gravity wheel, though for its smaller size the rate of spin could only be one spin per minute. To ensure that during long trips there was some amount of gravity in the ship, this specific mechanism was added in Space Tiger. The wheel also had additional living space and a secondary control room.

"There is, but it is not initiated very often to save

energy," Larisa said. "There is no artificial gravity in the saucer module. That's why we need to wear this suit all the time."

Taz shrugged. The suits looked nice and slick. He had no problem wearing one.

The space suits were thin, elastic to the touch. The boxy big space suits that were used in the initial stages of space exploration were long gone. With the progress in nanotechnology these areas had enjoyed immense improvement. Taz knew this type of gravity suits could provide some sense of gravity, though weak. When used with the gravity carpet it created more Earth like feeling, but still wasn't same. The idea was to have something workable. It was believed that living in a gravity free environment could cause bone loss to human body.

"Choose any one," Larisa said. "I'll put on mine and wait for you in the cockpit."

She left closing the door behind her. Taz quickly put on a green space suit. He hurried out of the cabin and took the elevator to the floor above. He found rest of the members of the team in the cockpit. Pete was there as well along with Dan.

Taz found Pete pretty much same as the images that he had seen of him in various magazines. He was about six feet tall with pale skin and light golden hair. He had a face with strong jaws, soft eyes and effortless smile – many would consider him handsome. He walked to Taz and shook hands cordially. "I am really happy to see you. Dan is always full of praises for you. I heard that you are very good at flying. Now you'll have to prove it to me. Simulations and reality are not the same."

"I flew real spaceships," Taz quickly mentioned. While most of his experiences were with simulated flights, he had had the opportunity to fly actual spaceships, though much smaller in size.

Pete burst into laughter. "I know. I know. I was just pulling your leg. Have you met everybody else?"

Taz shook his head. "No."

"They were changing," Larisa said. "I'll introduce him now."

A pretty young woman with brownish hair was smiling all along; she became the first one to get introduced.

"That's Michelle," Larisa said. Taz already knew BSD procedure was not to use last names for safety reason.

Michelle smiled moving her neck gracefully, creating a pleasant wave in her bob cut hair, and shook hands with Taz. "I am a Space Detective and the assistant captain of this ship. I have heard a lot of good things about you from Dan. Very glad to meet you."

"So am I," Taz shyly said. He liked Michelle readily.

Gentle, nice, friendly. It was impossible not to like her.

The stout, strong looking young man with dark hair standing beside Michelle stepped ahead and introduced himself. "I am Jason, from Australia. I am a Space Detective. You are from Dhaka, right?"

Taz shook hands with him. He had hard stone like hand, strong. It was difficult to believe that he was still a teenager. "Yes, I am. Have you ever been there?"

"Yes, I have. Very crowded place but I liked it. Lively," Jason said in a serious tone. Taz readily knew Jason was not the smiling type, but he was good at heart.

The last member of the team was a Chinese boy named Jing Jing. As the introduction started, he took out a small computer from his pocket and started to work on it. Larisa had to call him three times before he snapped out of whatever he was doing. "What?" He sounded clueless.

"Don't you want to introduce yourself to Taz, big shot?" Larisa teased.

At first Taz thought Jing Jing could be English challenged, but he proved him wrong. "Sorry. I have been trying to solve this mathematical puzzle for some time now," he said in perfect English. "Suddenly a clue popped up in my mind. I was just trying it out. And yes, I have heard about Taz. A little too young, but he would make a good Space Detective someday. What do think?"

He looked at Larisa for approval, who broke into a giggle fit. Jing Jing was skinny with straight black hair cut short, medium height, and wore round glasses. Taz didn't know people still wore glasses in this century. Practically everybody went for laser operated procedures to take care of such nagging issues. Jing Jing looked distant and absorbed. It was obvious in his mind he was still exploring the mathematical solution. He was probably fifteen-sixteen.

"You are not that old yourself," Larisa said after laboring to stop her giggle. "Taz, he is also a Junior Space Detective." Jing Jing just shrugged and went back to his work at hand. He didn't bother to shake hands. Taz understood he was a little outlandish.

Dan was discussing something with Pete quietly. He turned to Taz. "I know this is going to be your first trip to deep space, but don't worry a bit. You are already very much aware of Pete's reputation. Once you are up in the space, don't forget to call home and speak to your parents, or they would make my life miserable. Promise?"

Taz chuckled. "Promise."

"Taz, do you really want to be a Space Detective?" Pete asked.

"That is my only dream," Taz confidently said. "The first time my uncle mentioned about Space Tiger, I wanted to be a part of it. Finally my dream is coming true."

Pete smiled. "We are also very happy to have you with us. You are going to learn a lot in this trip. I have promised Dan that I'll bring you back safely. But you'll have to be obedient. I am the Captain Detective of this ship. It is mandatory to follow my commands. You must always remember that."

Taz nodded. "Yes, I know that. You won't have any problem with me."

"I am quite sure of that," Pete said. He looked at others. "We'll start in half an hour. Everybody please take your seat."

His instructions were followed immediately. Everybody took their respective seats before the lighted panels jammed with hundreds of switches, buttons and levers and was quickly lost into routine activities. It was clear, there were set of tasks assigned to each of them before taking off.

Dan shook hands with Pete, reminded Taz again to call home at his earliest convenience after taking off, and then stepped out of the spaceship.

All the exuberant ideas that Taz had in his mind about the taking off of such a big spaceship proved to be totally wrong. Sitting in his seat, Taz were checking out the functionality of the components on the control panels and didn't even notice how half an hour had passed.

"Time to fly,' Pete announced on the microphone.

"Five minutes."

Taz startled momentarily. How such a huge spaceship could be flown into the space was still a puzzle to him. As far as he knew, all the space bound rockets were sent out of atmosphere using booster rockets. Once in the space, they used their own engines to fly. But he had read Space Tiger used a different technology and didn't use the regular booster rockets.

"No boosters, right?' Taz asked Larisa who sat right next to him, quietly.

"No, no," Larisa said. "Space Tiger uses a new type of powerful engine. No booster is required."

"One minute," Pete announced in his usual soft voice.

Taz noticed a number of belts from under his seat snaked out and tied him to the seat. These were seat belts. Was there going to be lot of shakes and jerks? He was about to ask Larisa but decided not to. He had already asked too many questions. She might get fed up. Larisa must have read his mind. She smiled. "Don't worry. The ship is very smooth. You won't even feel a thing."

"How do you know? You never flew into it," Taz said.

"I heard. It's going to be okay."

# Chapter 3

Taz didn't even hear or feel the engine start. The Cockpit must have been very well sound proofed. He had never experienced such silent take off. All he felt was a slight trembling under his feet. Habitually, he turned his head and tried to look out through the windows, but soon noticed that all of them were fully covered. All he could see was the blue sky on the monitor. Several moments passed by quietly. The shaking under the feet stopped. The sound of the engine could be heard like a humming. The monitor showed they were heading through the atmosphere to the space. Speed was comparatively less – only 11 kilometers (7 miles) per second. Hundred years ago the rockets used to travel in such slow speed. Now there was nothing that flew less than 48 kilometers (30 miles) per second, not to Taz's knowledge. He couldn't be sure how this spaceship hoped to travel to Mars. Even when Mars was closest to earth the distance was 56 million kilometers (35 million miles). At its farthest it was 400 million kilometers (250 million miles) away. Fortunately, at this time of the year Mars was closest to Earth. That's why this was the time when tourists flocked in Mars into numerous resorts that mushroomed there. Taz had read so much about these resorts that he always wanted to visit them. He had never thought his wish would come true so quickly.

"Why are we moving so slowly?" Taz asked Larisa.

The answer, however, came from Pete, who must have overheard him. "Good question. If we try to go too fast with a spaceship of this size through our atmosphere we'll be spending too much energy. That's why Space Tiger flies very slowly for the first few hundred kilometers. Later we'll gradually increase the speed. How is your suit working? Do you have feelings of gravity?"

Taz hadn't paid much attention to his space suit. Now that Pete mentioned, he noticed he wasn't feeling as weightless as he expected to. He wondered how it would feel when they went further up in the space.

On a section of the monitor the Earth became visible. It looked like a bluish green ball floating in a thick white cloud. What a beautiful view that was! Taz had already seen this spectacular view several times, but it never failed to amaze him.

"Are you homesick?" Pete asked.

Taz felt awkward. He could see everybody else smiling at him. This was really his first time going so far away from Earth leaving his family behind. He did feel a little bad. Mars wasn't particularly next door neighborhood. So much could happen there. He felt some sort of vacuum inside him, especially for his parents. Both of them were so caring and loving! His mother was against this all along. Uncle Alam and Dan worked hard to convince her.

"Do you want to talk to home?" Pete asked.

Taz shrugged. That didn't seem like a bad idea. Pete touched his shoulder mildly in an assuring way. "There's nothing to be ashamed of. Go to your cabin. Use the monitor to call home. Once you are done, return to cockpit."

Taz wasted no time to get to his cabin. Using the controls in the monitor he had no problem calling home. His parents must have been waiting because the phone was picked up almost instantly. The two brothers came huddling. Seeing his whole family sitting right in front of the video receiver, Taz had hard time controlling his tears. He was an emotional kid. He tried not to show but deep inside he was.

"Son, are you up in the orbit now?" Mom sounded very worried.

"Not in the orbit, mom," Taz laughed. "We are heading for the true space. We are now about 7000 kilometers (4500 miles) away from earth."

"To me that makes no difference dear. Orbit and that true space thing are both away from home. When will you reach Mars?"

"At the speed we are going now, it could take us months."

"I heard Space Tiger moves in super speed," dad gravely said.

"Bro, they must have put you in a different ship," His younger brothers teased. "It's not Space Tiger. Ha…ha…ha…"

"Don't be silly!" Taz rebuked. "Captain told me the speed is increased gradually. At full speed we'll be moving 500 kilometers (~300 miles) per second. But I really don't know when we'll be moving at full speed."

"500 kilometers per second!" His brothers screamed. "Bro, you are so lucky!"

Taz kept the conversation short. He wanted to go back to the cockpit. He didn't want to waste time in his cabin on the first flight he had in Space Tiger. He said bye to everybody and quickly returned to the cockpit. As he took his seat, he noticed on the monitor that they were now about 10,000 kilometers (~6000 miles) away from earth. Looking at the earth shrouded by the hovering clouds, he felt a strange love for the planet. Billions of people lived there coping up with love, hatred, pain, sufferings, and happiness. Looking from the space one would never guess any of that.

"Let's slowly increase our speed," Pete softly instructed. "Our spaceship has the ability to move at 500 kilometers per second. But we won't be able to get to that speed too quickly. We'll have to get there gradually. Michelle, please turn on the nuclear engine."

"Starting the nuclear engine," Michelle repeated the instruction. She became busy on the control panel before her. After a few seconds they could see on the monitor that their speed was increasing... twenty... thirty...forty...soon they touched 150 kilometers mark. It didn't stop there. They continued to accelerate at the same rate. Taz could not believe that they were moving so fast!

Most of the functions in the ship were automatic. In case of any problem, one of the numerous alarm systems would caution the crew about it and would also instruct on the type of response it required. If necessary, technicians on Earth could help resolving issues remotely.

After a little while Michelle and Jason left their seats and walked at the back of the cockpit where they sat at a table. Larisa, Jing Jing and Taz also followed them after a little hesitation. They weren't sure if that would be okay or not. Larisa was the first one to follow the footsteps of Michelle and Jason. Jing Jing appeared to follow her unconditionally. They sat at a table and invited Taz. Unsure about what to do Taz looked at Pete, who smilingly nodded with his approval.  By the time he joined them Jing Jing was already totally consumed drawing doodles on his computer screen. Larisa affectionately said, "Don't you dare bother him. He is doing something very important, as always."

"Don't be silly!" Jing Jing protested. "I am just doodling. It's not important. Or maybe it is. It might help me solve the complex mathematical problem that I am working on. Something might pop up in my mind. Very few mathematicians in the world have been able to solve that one. I am pretty close, but can't get to the end of it."

"Don't waste time talking," Larisa joked.

"Don't bother me!" Jing Jing weakly protested.

Taz had already learned from Larisa that she and Jing Jing had flown together for a few times. Both had immense interest in engineering and were studying on nuclear engines. Not everybody got the opportunity to work with Pete. He had selected them to be part of this trip based on their excellent grades and high recommendations. No doubt CI-6 had played an important role in it. He had always been aggressive to create opportunities for the young and talented people.

Taz noticed Pete hadn't moved from his seat at all. He had been diligently doing something on the control panel in front of him. Michelle and Jason had been talking quietly. It didn't take a genius to figure out that they were more than colleagues. Moreover, Larisa had already revealed quite a bit about them. According to her, some of it was in the tabloids. Taz found it quite interesting. Who had ever thought that the tabloids would be interested in Space Detectives? This felt good. Public interest was always a positive thing. The only problem was, tabloids usually wrote based on rumors and false information. That wasn't good for BSD. It simply had no room for negative publicity. A lot of money was at stake.

Taz didn't realize he was staring at them. Larisa nudged him lightly. "Show some respect," she whispered. "Don't stare."

Taz felt truly ashamed. At his age curiosity could be a killer, he admitted to himself. He quickly looked at the central monitor to focus his attention somewhere else. The spaceship was moving at a velocity of 350 kilometers per second. They were still accelerating at the same rate as before. Pete must have noticed the awe in his face. He left his seat and joined them. "Space Tiger is not just another spaceship. As you already know, we are capable of going pretty fast. Though, if you ask me, in comparison to speed of light, 500 kilometers per second is not that fast. Still, we have a great technology, which can only get better. Are you wondering how it is done?"

"Nuclear reactors!" Taz said. "But I read even with a nuclear reactor the velocity couldn't be more than 160 kilometers per second."

"Good point. There was a limitation. However, Space Tiger uses some additional technology to overcome that. See, the limitation was not with the engine, but with the propellant that was used to control the speed. It wasn't the best. But with the invention of a specific type of gaseous mixture, we have been able to improve that."

"Hopefully someday we'll be able to go much faster than this," Jing Jing mumbled.

"Why, it is not fast enough for you?" Larisa teased.

Jing Jing shrugged indifferently.

"At this speed it shouldn't take us too long to reach Mars," Taz said, happily.

"Two days, max," Pete said. "This is your first time into the deep space, right?"

"Right. I have never gone beyond earth's orbit before."

Pete patted his back gently. "Do you really want to be a space detective? It is not an easy job. One can never relax. Michelle and Jason know that very well," he said, loud enough for Michelle to hear. She gave away one of her sweet smiles.

"But it's pretty interesting. Makes one feel very important," She said.

"I love it too," Jason added. "I had always wanted to be an astronaut, but never did I imagine that I would end up being a Space Detective. Thanks to you Pete. You picked me."

"Don't thank me. I picked you because you were

smart. I saw something special in you. Dan wants me to take experienced, older detectives. I don't want to do that. My goal is to build a generation of young Space Detectives, who would one day become the future leaders of this organization. Folks who had been around for too long are into it for just money and reputation. They are not helping the interest of BSD. Anyway, I rather not discuss about that now. Michelle's dad is one of the directors of this organization, so she knows some."

"Dad sometimes says, if things keep moving the way it is now, one day it would become a privately owned organization," Michelle said.

"What that would mean is, all the reputation that this organization had achieved as a neutral force, would evaporate quickly." Pete didn't look happy at all.

"But I thought BSD was the best organization in the whole world," Larisa said. "Why would they allow it to go to private ownership?"

"Good point, Miss Larisa," Pete smilingly said. He had a big brother like affection for Larisa, something that he did not even try to hide. "The problem is most countries do not contribute to carry the expenditure in keeping this organization up and running. Only a handful of rich countries with special interest, pay the tag. If the company executives decide to put this organization for private ownership, I doubt they'll face much objection."

"But in that case, how would this organization continue?" Taz asked. "Will a private organization have enough money to run this operation?"

"Excellent question!" Pete said. "The fact is, even today a large portion of the total funding for this organization comes from private sector. You already know that many private companies are now opening up all kind of businesses in the space – from moon to Mars. Most of them are trying to catch rich tourists. Some others are trying to dig out valuable metals and looking for convenient ways to bring them to earth. In total, there can be as many as several million people living temporarily away from earth. The major task for the Space Detectives is to investigate and apprehend criminals who cause trouble in those temporary space neighborhoods. But remember, we are not cops. We only get engaged when a country or a company send request for service. Almost like private detectives. As a result, almost all the expenses are carried on by the clients. That is why even if the organization becomes fully private there should be no issue with funding."

"Which company on Mars asked for us this time?" Jason asked.

"Big Earth Enterprise. Enormous company. They have several operations running both on Earth and in the space. They have a big tourism business in Mars. Around this time of the year as Mars comes very close to Earth, many tourists go to visit it. Three days ago, two of their tourists disappeared from an attraction site. They are guessing it could be a case of kidnapping."

"This makes it the fourth time in just one year," Jing Jing said without looking away from his computer. "The space is turning out to be another turf for the criminals, I guess."

Pete agreed. "Jing Jing is right. Men are travelling to space for a while now but there had never been so many incidents of kidnapping in a single year. I am with the BSD for about six years. I haven't seen anything like this."

Taz did a quick calculation in his mind and was quite surprised to find out that Pete had been leading such missions since he was only sixteen! That was awesome!

A mechanical voice spoke out from Captain's panel. It was CI-6. Pete stood up. "Time to provide a status. You guys can go back to your cabins. If you prefer, you may hang around in the cockpit as well. Michelle is our food minister. If you are hungry let her know and she might bless you with some delicious treats."

Michelle chuckled. "You always exaggerate. All the foods are cooked and right in the refrigerator. I just heat them up when required."

Pete grinned before returning to his seat. Taz noticed Jason had suddenly become a little gloomy. It wasn't hard to see that Pete and Michele shared a good friendship. Was Jason jealous? As he met Larisa's eyes, she winked. What did that mean? Was he right? May be he needed to start reading some of those tabloids.

Minutes later Michele left her seat. "Okay, if I am supposedly the food minister then let me serve the team. What do you guys want?"

"Ice cream!" Jing Jing showed some unusual excitement.

"Same for me too," Larisa echoed.

Michelle looked at Taz, who nodded. Jason did not care to respond.

So, ice cream it was. This was Taz's first food in Space Tiger.

# Chapter 4

Taz didn't even notice how two days had passed by. Usually there weren't a whole lot to do in a spaceship beside scientific researches. As they weren't involved in any such activities, at first it might seem that they would have difficulties passing time. In reality it was just the opposite. Having several young people on board created a party like environment. Passing time was not a problem.

Space Tiger was primarily controlled by the autopilot. Pete only checked every now and then. He spent some time to provide training to the three youngest members. Taz had the opportunity to check out how to fly this behemoth. Even though there were millions of mechanical and electrical parts, only a few could be controlled using switches, buttons, and levers located on the control panel. In some cases voice commands could be used as well. Normally autopilot controlled all of those. Manual override was possible but rarely done. From experience it was observed that machine showed better skill in flying than humans.

The crew cabins were on the smaller side, making it difficult to have a gathering there. So the team had spent most of the time on the cockpit. Pete seemed to be a party loving guy. He knew lot of jokes and made everybody laugh until their belly ached. Michelle knew ghost stories. She dimmed the light on the cockpit and said all kind of scary stories. Larisa talked about Brazil. She was from Brasilia, capital of Brazil. She had endless stories to say about her city. Taz said things about Dhaka. Despite its overcrowding and plethora of problems the city had its magical sides as well. Jason wasn't good at story telling. He didn't seem to have much sense of humor either. Laughing at a joke was not something that came easily for him. The only person who did not care a bit about all this was Jing Jing. It seemed as if his life depended on solving that math problem.

As they closed on to the destination, Pete called a meeting and briefed them. "You must already know all this but I need to repeat – don't go outside controlled environment when you are in Mars. The gravitational force there is one third of Earth's and the air is quite different than ours. It has very little oxygen. You won't last very long without proper suit."

"What is going to happen once we reach Mars?" Larisa asked.

"Our host company would receive us from the dock of the space station. They'll arrange for our boarding, meals and other needs while we stay there."

"When are we going to start our investigation?" That was Jing Jing.

"Looks like you are holding your breath for that," Larisa teased.

"I like to investigate," Jing Jing tried to defend himself.

Larisa gave him a friendly slap at the back. "Chill! I am just kidding."

Pete smiled. "Don't worry. That is the reason we came all the way here. There will be plenty of time for that. Though it is hardly anything like what you read in the story books. One might even say it's sort of boring."

Michelle laughed. "And you are still at it."

"I like it. I know you don't like it that much. But you are pretty good as an investigator. You have good observations. Better than mine."

"You are always exaggerating," Michelle shyly said.

"He is right," Jason added with his usual graveness.

"Landing in five minutes," autopilot announced in deep voice.

Pete signaled everybody to take their seats. The seatbelts wrapped them up automatically as before. The ship was slowing down, they felt it. Looking out through the windows they could see the red planet of Mars far away in the space. Taz was mesmerized. Seeing something in a picture and looking at it face to face was quite the different experience.

All the windows were covered before they entered the atmosphere of Mars. This was done as protective measure. The Space Tiger landed almost silently in a dock completely surrounded by tall walls.

After ten minutes Pete shut off the engine and left his seat. Others followed him. They went back to their respective cabins and changed cloths. Most resorts in Mars had average to pretty good artificial gravity and no special suits were required.

A little later, they all gathered in the hallway next to the cockpit. Pete cleared his throat to get their attention. "Listen team, I have a few very important things to share. Number one, we did not come here for a pleasure trip. We are on the job. What that means is that we must always be alert. Do not go anywhere unless you have to. Curiosity is good but controlling it is even better.

"Number two, don't forget someone or some group have kidnapped two of the tourists. My guess is they are nearby. They may already know or will soon know about our arrival. They must have informants in the resort. We may get attacked. We must be very careful.

"Number three, Gary Lester is the CEO of Big Earth Enterprise. Many considers him as a two faced snake. We must not disclose any information about our investigation to him or to any of his employees. Clear team?"

"Clear," everybody echoed.

"Any question?"

They all shook heads. This was the first time in Mars for all of them except Pete. It didn't need telling that they were all dying to get out of the spaceship and on to the Mars. Pete smiled. "Just remember all the things that I said. Taz, you are the youngest member of the team. You must stay with me."

With the touch of a button the big sliding door silently moved aside. They stepped into the waiting elevator. It zoomed down forty feet to the ground level. A middle aged white man was waiting to receive them. He was six three-four, well built, instantly gave an impression that he worked out on regular basis. His confident movement showed sign of power and strength. He extended his hand to Pete. "Hello Pete. I haven't met you before but I have heard a lot about you. Dan thinks someday you would become a legend as a Space Detective." He spoke slowly in a deep voice.

Pete shook hands. "Gary Lester?"

"Call me Gary. Your team?" he gestured at the rest.

Pete introduced his team members to Gary. It was obvious that he (Gary) had already received all the information about his guests. He shook everybody's hand, called them by first name and cordially said "Welcome to

City of Mars". Once introduction was over, Gary showed them the way out of the dock.

"What has happened here is very significant," he said as they all followed him. "That's why I did not send anybody else to receive you. I made it a point to come myself. I have already made all the arrangements for your stay. Once you have time to settle down, one of my men would come and take you to the spot where the incident had happened. Two of my guards will be staying with you all the time. I don't expect anything bad to happen but it's good to be on the safe side. Do you have any weapons with you?" the last question he threw at Pete.

"Just regular laser guns," Pete said. "Only Michele, Jason, and I carry them. Rest are unarmed."

"We don't usually allow any of the guests to carry arms," Gary said. "If anybody brings them we store the weapons during their stay. They get them back before leaving the city. However, I have decided to make an exception. Your weapons will not be confiscated. Dan already informed me that you might carry a few weapons."

Gary stopped before a door and put his face close to a glass panel. The door opened instantly. As they stepped out in the specious lobby they were stopped by three robot guards. Robots like these had been in use for a while now. Many companies were building them. They ranged from very basic to highly efficient. In most cases they were given regular human like appearances. One could still figure out their identity, but not readily. For some reason these three guards were huge, fearsome, and very mechanical looking. Gary sensed the surprise in their eyes. "Fear factor!" he said.

"Paper please!" one of the guards rudely asked.

"They are with me," Gary said.

The guard looked at Gary with a blank face and then looked back at the visitors. "Are you carrying any weapons?"

Pete, Michelle and Jason nodded. The first guard signaled the other two. They walked to them and took the laser guns, examined them briefly, and returned to their owners. It was obvious that they took images of the guns, scanned the serial numbers, and uploaded all that information in a central database. These were very modestly powered laser guns, but could kill or damage nonetheless though their primary function was to make the enemy immobile. They had a special function to generate laser rays in a particular frequency, which could shock a human body, or even robots, into a state of lethargy for ten to twenty minutes. However, such technology was still at infancy and confidence was low. Hence, it also had an alternate state when it worked as regular laser guns. In its deadly form, it could easily burn through a human or robot body.

Next, the guards quickly patted all of them including

the unarmed members. Gary allowed it. That underlined his concern about safety. It was not customary to have BSD members go through such procedures. Pete didn't like it but he didn't object. It was Gary's city. He had the right to set up the policies. Once checking was completed a temporary electric tag was implanted on their arms. "Duration one week," the chief guard said. "If you want to stay beyond that the duration must be extended."

"There are many kiosks in the city," Gary added. "You can just go to one of them and apply for extension. I'll make sure that I approve them in advance. Pete, you are familiar with that process. Please explain it to your team members. Not getting timely extension can cause unnecessary trouble. Our work here is done. Let's go."

The guards quietly moved aside. They walked across the lobby to a long corridor. At the end of this corridor there were several elevators next to each other. They took one and went up to the first floor. They were taken by surprise as they stepped out of the elevator. Right ahead stood a city with an artificial roof soaring several hundred feet above ground, neatly built web of roads, large commercial buildings, and beautiful residential areas. At a distance was the ominous transparent wall of the city that surrounded it completely almost like an eggshell. They could see the dry, barren, rough red land of Mars outside the shell.

"Wow!" Taz could not hide his amazement. He had known about City of Mars but never thought it was that big.

"The great City of Mars!" Gary said with a touch of detectable pride. "It was my company that made the dream of building cities in Mars a reality. I spent at least forty years of my life in this project."

"The gravity feels same as in earth!" Jing Jing noticed first.

Gary shrugged. "Close to it, not exactly same. We created gravitational force underneath this city, artificially. That was a very difficult task. We had to improve the existing technology, bring in all kind of instruments, what an experience that was! There is our car."

A black limousine approached silently and stopped next to them. A big young man opened the driver side door and stepped out. "Sorry boss, I am slightly late. Miss Mila was playing video games. I kept on calling her but she wouldn't come. She does not listen to anything I say."

"Rico!" a sharp female voice screamed out. Moments later a girl in her early teen climbed out of the car. She was skinny but looked strong, had a pretty face with restless eyes. Her long black hair was tied in two pony tails. She wore a colorful knee long skirt and a thick crème color pullover. Even with her face twisted in anger, she looked prettier than any girl Taz had ever set his eyes on. He could not move his eyes of her. He almost knew Larisa smirking at him, but he felt hypnotized. Who had ever thought that he would meet the prettiest girl ever so far away from earth!

"You talk too much," she barked at Rico. "I was doing something very important."

"You were playing video games! That was not important," Rico solemnly said.

"You are not my dad. Don't talk to me like that."

"I am your guardian. Boss, what do you say?"

Gary laughed loudly. "Are you guys just going to fight or welcome our guests here? Mila, you are always talking about Pete. Here is that famous Detective Pete."

Mila blushed. "Oh! You are the great Pete! You know what – I want to be a Captain Detective just like you. Good to meet you."

Pete shook her hands. "It would be a pleasure to have you in BSD. Let me introduce my team to you."

Mila barely paid any attention but did wave to them. There was an air of recklessness in her attitude. She didn't seem to care about what others thought about her.

"Please hop in the car," Gary said with some urgency. "We shouldn't be standing here like this. Things are changing here. My own city, but I can't say it is safe anymore."

Once everybody boarded the car Rico pulled away.

As they went through busy streets they were charmed by the hundreds of colorful, flashy stores that flanked both sides of the roads. It looked and felt almost like a tourist town somewhere in North America. The only thing that gave away its true identity was the transparent shield around the city that provided a glimpse of the gray Mars sky.

"Do you get a lot of tourists here?" Taz asked hoping to start a conversation with Mila.

Mila looked at him with pure annoyance. "Why, don't you read magazines? The whole world knows about City of Mars. It's peak time for tourism. Everyday thousands of visitors are coming. Keep your eyes on the right. Our space shuttle port is located little ahead. Everyday at least a dozen ship arrives there."

"After a few months it would slow down," Rico added.

"Who asked you to talk? Always interrupting," Mila scolded.

"You are becoming too skittish. We'll have to send you for some counseling," Rico said, maintaining his usual calmness.

Gary laughed. Clearly enjoying their childish quarrel.

"Are all the other cities on Mars as big as this?" Michelle asked.

"No. Of course no," Gary quickly responded. "There

are a handful of other places on Mars that can claim to be a city, but they are neither as big nor as beautiful. Ask Pete. He had the opportunity to see a few of them."

"I totally agree," Pete said, "I have been to a couple of others. Both were much smaller with weaker gravity. The overall comfort was far less."

"Is there a way to commute between different cities?" Larisa asked.

"We have underground trains. There are also private planes," Gary said. "In last five years things has taken off here. The way tourists are flocking, it is only a matter of time before hundreds of resorts mushroomed. There will be more crimes, troubles, agony. We'll leave no place in this universe in peace." Gary sounded bitter, clearly not looking forward to such unwelcome competition.

"Do all the resorts have their own cities?" Taz asked.

"Are you nuts?" Mila retorted before Gary had a chance to respond. "Do you have any clue how much money it takes to build a city like this? Do you think every schmuck have that much money?"

Taz got a little nervous. Why was this girl always on the edge?

"Don't mind her," Rico said. "Some of the existing resorts actually do have their own small cities. The tourists can also visit cities located in other resorts."

"For a fee," Gary said. "We receive a lot of visitors from other resorts. We had to come up with a strategy to manage the flow. Running a city of this size is not cheap. Once we introduced visiting fees the other resorts have followed us too. Anyway, look at your right. That's our public space shuttle port."

The port was clearly visible through the transparent wall. It was several kilometers long and equally wide. Eight to ten spaceships were parked at different points. They could see people walking in and out from a few of them.

"I had no idea so many people come to Mars," Jason sounded surprised.

"The financial institutions on earth now provide travel loans. Many people do not want to lose such an opportunity to visit Mars," Gary said.

"We didn't land there, did we?" Larisa asked.

"No," Pete answered. "There is another port for private spaceships, on the other side of the city."

"How many space ports like this are there on Mars?" Jing Jing asked.

"Which universe did you guys come from?" Mila snapped. "Do you know how much investment is required to build a port like this? Jeez!"

Gary laughed out loudly. "That's my daughter! A total bully but with many virtues."

"Be quiet, dad!"

Gary continued to laugh as if she had said something really funny. Mila gave him an angry look but didn't say anything.

# Chapter 5

Rico dropped Gary and Mila to their house and drove Pete and his team to a big hotel named *The Martians*. On the way he revealed his true identity, little boastfully. He was a very sophisticated robot – a top of the line in the Smartman model, the most intelligent robots ever made. This surprised everybody. It was impossible to figure out just by talking to him. Rico seemed proud of the facts that he could think and do things much faster than a human brain. His body, made of specially developed bio-mechanical substance, was also much stronger and disease resistant than human body. Moreover, he was charming for a robot, good mannered and had a decent sense of humor.

"If we could turn all humans on Earth to robots like this then we would be better off," Larisa whispered into Taz's ear. "We could program everybody to be good. There would be no crimes."

The hotel was exuberant with one minor issue, the guest rooms were on the smaller side. This was done intentionally to accommodate more guests in a smaller area. Each one of them was given a separate room, but they didn't have much time to spend there. It was already late afternoon. Pete wanted to visit the crime scene before nightfall. Local robot guards had collected some information, which was sent to him in advance. He shared all that information with rest of the team. Data processors had shrunk greatly and now could easily fit in a half inch by half inch box. Many people carried them in their pockets. When there was a need to compose a message it could be vocally recorded, or be done using thought plug-ins. The personal devices could be tuned to a particular frequency allowing them to be connected to an individual. Collecting and sharing information had become really easy.

Rico became their chauffeur, guide, as well as the security guard. He brought some food for them from the Hotel Cafeteria and carried it into the limousine. Once he assured that he would clean up any mess before Gary rode the car everybody dived on the food. They were hungry and the food was hot and appetizing. Having a meal so good so far from Earth was something memorable for Taz. City of Mars definitely had some really good cooks.

Rico was taking them to the crime scene. It was in a location external to City of Mars. The plan was to drive to a train station and then take the train to the spot. The posted maximum speed limits were quite low with only 50 kilometers (30 miles) per hour allowed on the Highway Zero. The roads had decent traffic but nothing to hold up normal flow. This was a relief. Experiencing traffic jam in a small city, by earth's standard, would be hard to swallow. Rico shared that most residents hated the low speed limit, but who was going to take that on with Gary? The last thing he wanted was a spat of accidents on the streets of City of Mars. Low speed limit did work and kept the number of road accidents to very low numbers.

City of Mars was close to 10 kilometers (6 miles) long and little over a km (half a mile) wide. A four lane freeway – Highway zero – ran around the city almost flanking to the transparent boundary shell. Side roads merged into Highway zero in regular intervals. They noticed the side roads were named using numbers - side road 1, 2 etc. Any road that spawned from a side road was named after the side road along with a digit to specify its order, like side road 1-1, 1-2 etc. Gary had sent them a detail map of the City of Mars. One look at the map and it would become crystal clear that Gary wanted an oval shielded city with a highway running along the perimeter with streets crisscrossing in a nice neat pattern. Side roads that ran width wise were half a mile apart and merged into highway Zero on both ends. Side roads that ran lengthwise were only quarter of a kilometer apart and did not merge into the highway. They were called connecting roads.

Taz counted – there were in total eleven side roads and thirty connecting roads, considering each section between two side roads were counted as one, as they were named separately. The commercial establishments were built by the side roads and practically all the residential areas were located by the connecting roads. In total, about five thousand people lived in the city around the year, though none of them were officially permanent residents. They travelled back and forth, some once every six months, some once a year or longer. Thinking ahead for future, Gary had built apartment complexes ranging from three to ten stories. A small percentage of houses were detached two storied buildings, but were allocated for special guests only. Gary himself lived in one of these houses surrounded by highly secured boundary walls. He lived with his daughter, Mila. His wife did not want to accompany him to Mars. They were divorced long ago. Mila lived with her mother until she was twelve. After that, she travelled to Mars to be with her father. They learned from Rico that beside the intelligent robots generally known as Smartman, Gary and Mila were the only humans, who could claim to be permanent residents of this city.

Once the feeding frenzy ceased and everybody looked content, Pete opened his mouth for the first time since they boarded the limousine. Until now, he hadn't shared a lot about the assignment. Either he did not have all the information, or he wanted more time to think it out.

"Have you read the information that Gary sent?" he asked.

They had, several times. This was the report that Gary's robot detectives had created after conducting their own investigation.

Four days  ago, a team of tourists from City of Mars went for a guided tour to Black Hole Canyon – an attraction site about 30 kilometers (~20 miles) away from the city. They went there by underground train. Smartman - 10 was the only robot guard with that team. Just like the streets, all robots had a number, with the exception of Rico, of course. Two humans were assigned to the team as guides. One was the designated or main guide, while the other one was the backup guide, just in case the main guide couldn't make it. Tourists liked human presence. Most of the guides were human and came from different parts of the Earth. It was necessary to cater tourists from different regions, speaking different languages, and having distinct cultures. Over the years culturally blended societies had grown on Earth, but there had also been parallel efforts by many countries and localities to hold on to their own cultural inheritance by any means.

The Black Hole Canyon was a very deep canyon and was a popular tourist site. It had a large fully covered beautifully constructed viewing platform from where tourists could get a nice glimpse of the canyon and the surrounding area. For tourists, who wanted more, there were special small planes called *porter* that they could rent and go all the way to the bottom of the canyon. From that party, two tourists opted for that – a man and a woman. The fleet of small tourist planes, the porters, was operated by Smartman pilots. They were skilled pilots with little to no social skills.

The Canyon was about 8 kilometers (5 miles) deep at its lowest point. The two tourists flew at the bottom without any trouble. Once their porter landed, they had stepped out for a walk in the narrow canyon. This was customary and never had any incidents. During this particular trip, everything was going just fine. The pilot was in constant contact with the control room on the ground. Fifteen-twenty more minutes and they would fly back up. There was no indication of anything suspicious.

Suddenly something had happened. Ground lost contact with the porter. Twenty minutes had passed. Control was about to send a rescue mission, when the porter returned to the port. However, there were several problems: the tourists had disappeared; the robot guard was shot and disabled; the pilot and the human guide both suffered temporary memory loss.

Out of many things, what became the focal point was the fact that the pilot of the plane, Smartman – 119, could not remember anything at all about the incident. It appeared as if somebody or something had wiped of his memory for that particular time frame. He could remember everything before and after. He recollected of the part when the tourists climbed out of the plane. After that, complete blank. Following some hypnotic sessions, he vaguely remembered of seeing a flash of very bright light, but nothing else.

Gary had personally visited the spot with several guards. They did not see anything suspicious. There were no signs of struggles, fights or anything else, whatsoever. They saw or found nothing to take them any closer to find out what had happened to those tourists.

"How can this be possible?" Michelle said to Pete.

Pete shrugged. "I have no clue. Black Hole Canyon is a very popular location in this region. It's like a Mecca for all tourists, who come to visit Mars. But the percentage of visitors, who take the flight down is not very big. It is quite scary just to look from above. I have never heard of any trouble there. The security is tight, so there's little room for trouble anyway. At least two to three armed guards come from each of the resorts that offer guided tours to their patrons. And these are robots with James Bond like abilities. I have seen them in action. Regular people will have no chance to stand against them. Their biomechanical bodies also give them a clear advantage in Martian environment.

Anyway, according to this report, none of them had seen anything suspicious either."

"Are we going to get down to the bottom of Black Hole Canyon?" Larisa asked with a great amount of excitement.

"I don't see we have much choice," Pete said.

Jing Jing raised both hands in the air, surrendering. "I am not going anywhere near that place. Just thinking of it is making me shiver."

Pete looked at Taz. "How about you Taz? Are you coming?"

"Yes, Yes," Taz hesitantly said. Clearly he wasn't intending to get marked as a coward, but at the same time wasn't really sure if 8 kilometers down the Canyon would be much fun or not.

Michelle smiled. "We are all going down there, right?"

Pete shrugged. "That would be my first preference. But if Jing Jing is too uncomfortable, we would make an exception. Jason, how about you? Hope you have no fear of canyons."

Jason shook his head. He had no issues. That's how he usually was. He opened his mouth only when nodding and shaking was not sufficient.

"Did Gary tell you who those two tourists were?"

Rico spoke on the intercom. Was he listening to their conversations? No way to say.

"No. Are they famous or something?" Pete asked.

"Step daughter and her husband of American President," Rico said.

Pete was silent for a moment. "Really? They had no presidential guards with them?"

"Nope. They hid their real identity. Must have thought nobody would recognize them considering both are privacy freaks. They have rarely been seen with the president. If you ask me, I would be surprised if there are ten Americans, who know them."

"An American president has many enemies. They must know every member and relatives of the president," Jason said.

Pete nodded. "Specially the organized criminal groups. But how would they come here?"

"I wish we knew that," Rico said. "I am almost certain this is the job of one of the criminal groups. But there's no way to know which one. I can't even imagine how they could get here. Before a Martian visa is issued, a tremendous amount of checking is done. It's hard to believe that after such strict background check, anybody with a criminal record can pass through."

There was a silence for a moment. Rico lived here. If

he didn't have the answer, none did. The limousine moved ahead in a leisurely speed through the busy Highway Zero.

# Chapter 6

The underground train was not really awe inspiring. It was almost like an infant in comparison to the large underground train systems some of the cities on Earth had. The system was only a level deep with two lines running parallel to allow trains going on both directions. The trains were much smaller with each containing ten to twelve compartments. Every 10 to 15 kilometers, there were stations that allowed changing trains. It was quite evident that when these lines were built, the primary goal was to keep the cost low. In future, if a lot of people came to live in Mars then the underground train system could be enlarged, and the coverage extended, Rico shared. However, he thought it was an unlikely scenario. One of the sectors that could potentially accommodate many jobs on Mars was mining. The problem was, even though there were many mines in Mars it was not financially viable to dig them out and to send the product to Earth for consumption. The cost would be sky high. The only way to get that industry going was to find usage right on Mars. That would require a sizable population living permanently in the red planet. Unfortunately, earthlings still were not ready to commit living in Mars for the rest of their lives.

The underground train dropped them at the foot of the Black Hole Canyon. The all glass observatory was located right next to the canyon and was directly accessible from the station. They climbed up the stairs to the ground level and walked a short distance to reach the observatory. The first thing that they noticed was the large crowd – no less than several hundred people, people from all over the world. It looked like a large party with people wearing colorful, culturally representative clothing, speaking in their own tongues. It took no time to figure out that all of these people were different shades of rich. Most people on earth did not have the means to visit Mars. The cheapest two-week tourism package was two hundred grand in US currency. Just the trip back and forth took ten days. Most of the passenger rockets were nowhere nearly as fast as Space Tiger was.

Rico went through a group of guards to lead them into a glass room. "We'll have to board our flight from here – to go to the canyon floor. I had booked earlier. The porter should be here anytime."

There were several of those glass rooms standing next to each other.  Inside each of them waited several tourists, patiently. A batch of porters was out with tourists. Once they returned, they would unload, load up with new passengers and go off for another trip.

Outside the clear wall was a rough, dry land dotted

with tall mountains and deep canyons. Taz was stunned looking at the unparallel beauty of this rugged and exotic land. He could not find words to express his overwhelming feelings. He had watched several documentaries on Mars while on Earth that contained detailed views of many Martian attractions including the famous Black Hole Canyon. However, he felt it was quite different to see something on a visual media and in person. Even the best of the images could not show the enormousness and the depth of raw beauty that simply stood there lonely, melancholy but yet with such stubbornness.

He knew Mars had many canyons, some equally large and deep as the Black Hole Canyon. The primary reason for this canyon to become a popular tourist spot was due to its convenient location in the warmer part of Mars, where all the resorts were located.

They did not have to wait too long. Not even five minutes had passed, when a porter glided through air and silently landed on a tiny spot next to their glass room. They were rather small, shaped like a saucer with short tail and wings. They flew more like gliders, made very little noise, and could turn in the air very quickly. They were perfect for rough terrains. In Mars, a porter was essential for short trips inside the planet.

"Welcome in the porter number 61," as they boarded

the porter, the pilot, a Smartman, dryly announced.

"They are not particularly social type," Rico whispered.

The pilot must have heard it, because he gave Rico a hard look. Rico had no interest in getting into a confrontation. He looked away. The pilot switched on the engine, closed all the doors, and was getting ready to be airborne, when to everybody's surprise Mila rushed off the stairs and into the glass room, madly signaling them to stop.

"What do you want me to do?" The pilot asked Rico.

Rico shrugged. "We can't leave her behind. She would eat my head off."

The pilot shrugged too, almost sympathetically. Everybody seemed to know Mila here. These Smartmans definitely did. He opened the doors. Mila quickly climbed into the porter and slumped on a cushioned seat. "Let's go," She commanded, trying to catch her breath.

In thirty seconds the porter took off and slowly rose to a height of a hundred and fifty feet before moving ahead toward the canyon.

"I had no clue you wanted to come," Rico tried to sound apologetic.

"Don't bullshit me," Mila snapped. "You didn't want me to come. Do you think I am stupid?"

"Don't be silly!" Rico was calm. "Does boss know

you came?"

"He knows. I am the guide and you're the guard."

"I have to confirm. Boss didn't tell me anything." Rico reached for his phone.

"Do whatever you want, robot man!" Mila was out to hurt Rico.

Rico ignored it and called Gary up. They spoke briefly. Rico looked satisfied. He left Mila alone.

Pete grinned. "I like guides with attitude."

Mila gave him an annoyed look but didn't say anything. That's when Pete noticed a second porter was following them from a short distance. "Who are they?" He asked Rico.

"Extra guards. For your safety. Boss does not want to take any risk," Rico said.

"Don't be worried," Mila said. "I have high beam laser gun with me."

Pete felt little worried. A high beam laser gun could evaporate half of a person in one shot. He wasn't so sure if a young girl like her should be carrying such a powerful weapon. Mila must have sensed his concern. "Relax. I am a skilled gunner. I never miss."

That was even more worrisome, Pete thought. He looked at Rico, who nodded as if to reassure him.

The mountainous area was spread out for hundreds

of kilometers in all directions. There were many canyons scattered all around the region. The Black Hole Canyon was the closest and deepest. It was so deep that looking down from the edge one would see nothing clearly. The porter slowly started its journey down the canyon. Soon gray, faded rocky walls enveloped them from two sides. As they made it deeper, the rays of sun subsided considerably but still there were enough light to see. Pete looked back. The second porter was closely following. There were no other porters around. Gary must have had arranged it to make things more secure for them, he thought. It took them several minutes to reach the ground – all the way below. Once the porter landed on a small piece of flat land, they climbed out of it. The ground was rough and rocky but relatively plain. There were many cavern like deep holes in the rock walls, some of them were large enough to allow a vehicle ten times bigger than a porter to have a safe passage. Looking from outside, it wasn't readily clear whether the holes had a way out on the other ends or not.

"Couldn't somebody come through these holes and attack?" Michelle said.

"Only if somebody knows this area like the back of his hands," Pete said. "I would think many of these caves have no exit. Even if some do, how could you possibly know which ones?"

"A drone can be used to map them," said Jing Jing.

"Possibly," Pete agreed. He looked at Rico. "Is there any such map?"

"Nope," Rico shook his head. "What's the use? We never thought of doing it."

The second porter had landed nearby. Four Smartmans poured out of it and took positions around Pete and his team. They were all carrying high beam laser guns. Pete didn't think there was any real need for such measure. Who would be so stupid to attack them here? Anybody who had slightest idea about who Pete was would know that if anything happened to him BSD would hit back with all its might. There would be trouble, big trouble. Dan might even come himself.

They walked around for a little bit. Pete, Michelle and Jason took several pictures of the spot. There was nothing to suggest anything had happened there. They looked keenly through every inch of ground and nearby rock walls, but found nothing of interest.

"I came here just yesterday and looked around for a long time," Mila said, annoyed. "Didn't find a thing."

Rico shook his head quietly. It was obvious that he did not approve her coming here alone. But he managed not to say anything about it. Mila might snap.

Pete looked calm and composed as he continued to

take pictures of surrounding areas. Taz had taken some as well. He wanted to send them back home to his parents and siblings. This was his opportunity to let them all know that he was doing something very important here. Mila had already glared at him a few times but did not say anything yet. Taz felt a little alarmed. He was shy around girls. This girl looked so skittish that he was even scared to look at her, forget about starting a conversation.

After about twenty minutes, Pete asked to go back up.

"Did you get anything?" Rico asked.

"If we didn't find anything how would he?" Mila scoffed.

"She is right," Pete said. "There is no evidence here. Whoever did this, they were very careful. They had planned this for long time. They probably used Flash Memory Destabilizers to make the guard and the guide unconscious, and then forced the tourists into their porter. Nobody saw them getting out of here, which means they took one of these monstrous caves and got out of here through the other end, possibly several kilometers away."

Rico nodded. "That's possible. Those memory Destabilizers are bad dudes. Should we go back now?"

"There's not much we can do here," Pete said. "I have all the images I need to analyze later. Let's go back to the city."

They boarded the porter and flew back up to the observatory. As they walked down the stairs to the station, Mila looked pretty restless.

"Now what?" She asked. She wasn't looking at anybody specific but everybody understood it was for Pete.

"I am thinking of going to see somebody," Pete said, thoughtfully.

"Who? Smartman 10? The guard?" Jason said.

"I know he is disabled but still it may be worth taking a look. You never know what you can get from where," Pete said.

"Make sense," Michelle said. "No harm trying our luck."

Pete looked at Rico. "Do you think we can go check out the disabled guard?"

"Sure. Anything you want. Let's hop into the train. We have to go back to the City of Mars."

The next train took off in about ten minutes. They spent the time socializing and munching on some food that Rico got them from a food store. This was a large station with a mall, a decent sized food court, and even a small hotel. Something pleasant had happen there as they waited. Mila stroke up a conversation with Larisa and Jing Jing, something nobody thought she was capable of. She, however, showed little interest to the young boy who seemed to show a keen interest in her. This really hurt Taz. What did he do? Larisa noticed it and teased him relentlessly with her meaningful nudges and friendly pokes.

Once back in the city, Rico took them to a five storied building on side road 5 in the familiar limousine. There were several armed robots guarding the building. Rico nodded at the guards and walked through the heavy set of doors unchallenged. Rest of the team followed him. The guards observed them carefully but did not ask anything. Rico was a big shot here. The other robots in the city did not seem to have any desire to cross him. They walked through a short corridor and stepped inside a large room with high ceiling. A human worker greeted them. "This way please."

"I called ahead," Rico explained.

There were several metallic boxes with large drawers stood in a row alongside the walls. Each drawer was marked by a number. The man walked to a drawer and pressed a small button, which caused it to slide ahead silently. Guard number 10 was lying lifeless at the center of this drawer with a gaping hole in the head.

"Work of a high beam laser," The man said. "It has been retired. The cost to fix it is more than what it would take to buy a new one."

"Can you recover its memory?" Pete asked.

"Nope. The laser ruined most of his useful memory."

"What type of laser gun did this?" Michelle asked.

"High beam guns. Common stuff. Many of our guards use the same type of guns," The man answered. "Hard to distinct."

"I was thinking in the same line," Rico said. "Find the gun by looking at the damage done. I put couple of scientists on it. No luck. They couldn't come up with anything."

Pete took some pictures of the lifeless robot. A little later they started back.

"What's next?" Mila asked once they had all climbed into the car. "Smartman-119?"

"That seems like little more prospective. He is still breathing," Pete said, lightly.

"We tried a lot to talk to him - Dad and I," Mila said. "Had no luck. He couldn't say a thing. Didn't even know who he was. Total garbage."

"Too bad. I still have to try. May be I'll get lucky. Who knows?" Pete said as he started to walk back to the car.

Mila shrugged, did not say anything.

Rico drove them to side road 7. They parked in front of a three storied building. Well guarded but Rico and the team entered unobstructed. Inside it looked like a hospital or something of that nature with many robots of different models and shapes, most looked more or less damaged. Possibly a robot's hospital, Taz thought. They took the elevator to the third floor. Two smartman guards were guarding a room with high beam rifles. They moved aside to allow Rico and the team to enter the room. Pete assumed these robots had some kind of electronic way to identify Rico. This was a small room with little to no furniture. On the wall facing the door, there was a hook fixed to the wall. A Smartman was hanging from it. He had no sign of damages in his body but his eyes had this childish innocence, unusual for a robot. Clearly, something was not right about him.

"Smartman 119," Rico said. "His brain is fine but he can't remember a thing about the incident. Our robot scientists did some examinations and found that some of the active part of his memory is dead."

"Can I ask him some questions?" Pete asked.

"Sure. Knock yourself out. Just call him 119. He would respond."

"119!" called Pete. "I want to have a few words with you."

"Sure," 119 spoke normally. "But I won't be able to say anything about the kidnapping. I can't remember a thing about it."

"What is the last thing that you can remember?"

"We went down the Black Hole Canyon and landed on the floor without any trouble. Our guests stepped down to the ground and were walking away from us. That's when something must have happened, because I can't remember anything after that. Very abnormal."

"Were you unconscious?"

"Yes, I believe so."

"How long?"

"Can't be more than fifteen minutes. I saw the guard lying at the back seat, shot. The tourists gone. Didn't know what to do so I flew back to the port. Such event had never happened here. I was very surprised. And disappointed."

"Did you see anything suspicious?"

"Nothing suspicious. Everything seemed normal."

Pete had nothing else to ask. He inquired with others if they could think of asking anything else. When nobody showed any interest, Pete walked out of the room. Rest followed him.

"The Memory De-Stabilizer used here were pretty powerful," Pete said.

"I know," Rico said. "I have never seen anything like this before."

"Let's go talk to the guide," Mila said. "He definitely knows something."

"That poor guy is scared to death," Rico said. "I don't think talking to him would give us anything useful."

"You know nothing," Mila growled. "I am telling you Pete, this guy knows something."

Rico surrendered. "Okay, okay, we'll go." He turned to Pete. "He is in the bad side of the city, generally known as the entertainment district." Then to Mila, "If there is any kind of trouble I am not going to be responsible."

"Chicken!" Mila said. "Don't worry, Pete. As long as I am with you guys, you have nothing to fear."

Taz was about to chuckle, such high confidence seemed misplaced considering her age and size, but that was before Mila pulled out a ten inch high powered laser gun. He quietly swallowed it.

"There aren't too many gun hands as good as I am," Mila said, proudly.

Pete was concerned. Guns in the hands of kids were never a good thing. Skilled or not, in most cases they lacked in judgment, were too desperate to prove, often put others at risk. He hoped she wasn't going to do anything stupid. As his eyes met Rico's, he nodded, reassuring, once again.

They climbed back in the limousine and headed to side road 30 – a hub of night clubs, bars, and casinos. There were varieties of night clubs scattered all over the city, but a good number of them were concentrated in that part of the city earning it a reputation as the entertainment district. The neighborhood around Side road 30 was bright and heavily decorated. They were surprised to see the unusually large crowd and the party like environment.

"Wow, this looks like New York!" Larisa excitedly said. She was not yet old enough to get in a bar but was a big fan of dancing. She was waiting desperately to turn eighteen, when she would be allowed in a nightclub.

"I had no idea there was a place like this in this city!" Michele sounded excited.

"We haven't been in a club for long time," Jason said.

Michele nodded. "I wish we could dance a little."

"With the permission of the Captain....," Jason looked at Pete.

"I don't think that would be a smart thing to do," Pete shook his head. "A lot of people in this city probably know we are here. We don't know yet who are responsible for the kidnapping, but I am guessing they are not going to be happy about our presence. We can't take any risk. Sorry guys, another day."

Michelle and Jason smiled at each other.

"Yes, another day," Michelle murmured.

# Chapter 7

They drove past several big, flashing, noisy popular clubs and pulled in into a dimly lit parking lot with a lonely street light burning at the center. The building next to the parking lot was single storied, sprawling, and quieter with a large neon sign fixed to its roof that said 'The Terror'.

"Terrific name!" Jing Jing said.

"Terror my foot!" Mila muttered. Reason for her displeasure was not clear.

Unlike most part of the entertainment district, it was relatively barren with a handful of people, who gathered on the sidewalk talking rather quietly. The difference was so prominent that it was hard not to notice.

"This is the drugs land," Rico cleared things up.

"Really?" Pete said, surprised. "Gary has no problem with it?'

"Why should he? Half the people who come to visit us are either addicted or alcoholic. If they want to get high in a controlled environment, what's the problem? They don't cause problem, we don't bother them. On a side note, that's our bottom line."

"Who operates clubs like this?" Michele asked.

"Private companies from Earth. They pay a lot of

tax. Keeps Gary happy," Rico said.

"What happens if they don't pay?" Taz abruptly asked.

Mila gave him a hopeless look. Wasn't it a reasonable question, wondered Taz. The more he tried to impress the girl the worse it seemed to go. After that stupid question she was definitely thinking very low of him.

Rico laughed. "Don't forget this is Gary's city. All the guards in this city are either his property or on his payroll. He controls practically every aspect of life here. You can't cross him and still expect to do business in the City of Mars. And if you are not doing business here, you can't stay here. Simple equation."

"If they try to get smart, we kick their butt," Mila said with a smirk.

Taz continued to be amazed by Mila. A girl so young but spoke with such authority! Did life in Mars do it to her?

As they walked to the closed front gate, it silently opened up. A well built middle aged white man stepped out. "Rico! Didn't you just come yesterday and took all the information? What more do you need?"

"John, we need to speak to the guide one more time. We'll be quick," Rico said.

"Ron is not feeling very good. He has been a nervous wreck."

"I know. But we still need to see him," Rico insisted.

John recognized Pete. "Space Detectives! Looks like Gary got the best. Hello Pete! You don't know me but I know you. I heard lot of good things about you."

"Good to meet you," Pete briefly said. Neither of them attempted to shake hands.

"Can we come in?" Rico impatiently said. He made it clear they weren't going anywhere without seeing Ron.

"What other choice do I have?" John bitterly said as he moved out of the door. Inside, the light was dimmed, music played in low tune, men and women were sitting on sofas and chairs scattered all around a large hall room. Well dressed waiters and waitresses quietly moved around serving food, drugs, and drinks. They noticed three big men were standing right behind John. Humans. Their facial gestures gave them away.

Rico walked inside with the rest silently following him. John saw Mila a bit late. His face became hard. "See little girl, I don't want any trouble. I have no issues with your dad. I pay my dues on time. Never late."

"I'll be nice," Mila assured him. "Make sure your monkeys don't bother me. I don't like big monkeys."

"Can you ask her not to call us monkeys?" one of the men objected.

"What would you rather prefer? Pigs?" Mila snapped.

John raised a hand. "Okay, no need to get excited. What happened last time was a mistake. They didn't know who you were. Everything is good now." He looked at Rico. "You'll find Ron at the same room, all the way back. What a drag! He can't hang on to any job, that's why I put him there. Now look, what a mess I am in!"

Mila had no patience for chitchat. She kept on going. The main hall room was at least a couple of hundred feet long and was standing on three rows of pillars. They went across the hall room and stepped out into a wide corridor with access to several rooms. Ron was placed in a room right next to the exit. Rico knocked on the door. The door opened quickly. It was a small room with a double bed, a small table, and a pair of chairs. Ron was a big man but he looked very scared. He almost had a nervous breakdown at Rico's sight. "What do you want? I already told you I don't know anything. I can't remember anything. Why do you keep bothering me?"

John raised his hand, gesturing him to calm down. "Detective Pete has come with him. Just answer his questions. Nothing to worry."

Ron did not look happy at all. He suspiciously checked out Pete and the rest of the team. "What do you want to ask? I saw a very bright light. After that I can't remember a thing."

"Sit, Ron," Rico said. "There's no need to be so agitated. You know, the step daughter of the President has been kidnapped. That is not a very good thing and matter could get quite edgy. You understand that, don't you? We must rescue his daughter and her husband. Just tell us whatever you know."

"How many more times do I have to say that I don't know anything?" Ron sat on the bed heavily.

"I am Captain Detective Pete," Pete offered his hand to Ron but he did not make any attempt to take it.

"I just want to ask a few questions," Pete said. "Don't want to bug you for too long. The flash of the light that you saw, when did you exactly see it? Was it before the porter touched the ground or after?"

"After... after," Ron quickly said. "I was sitting at the back seat with the passengers. Suddenly this very bright light flashed. We all lost consciousness. When I woke up I was back at the center. I cannot remember anything in between."

"If you know nothing then why are you so afraid?" Mila sharply asked. "You definitely remember something. Either flush it out now or dad will come and beat it out of you."

"Rico!" John grudgingly said. "Please move her out of here. She is pure trouble."

"But she has a point," Rico said. "Why is your brother so scared?"

"It is quite easy to make a Smartman inactive by using the Memory De-stabilizer technology, as they are not programmed to back off on the face of danger," Mila said. "However, on the other hand, when faced with risky situations humans do not always jump into it right away and often take alternate route to avoid the immediate danger. I think Ron saw something suspicious and had already closed his eyes even before the flash of light took place. As a result, he did not have a memory lapse. You were probably pretending to be unconscious."

Ron started to shake. "I...I...didn't do any such thing. I am telling the truth."

There was a loud noise outside. Ron was so startled that he jumped out of the bed. "What was that sound?"

"I am checking," John said. His men were guarding the front door. There was something happening at the door but they could not see it from where they stood.

"Just tell us what you saw," Rico growled. "We don't have the whole day."

"I cannot remember anything," Ron answered looking away from him.

Mila stepped ahead and slapped him right on the face. "Are you kidding us? You were part of it. Do you want this city of ours to get ruined? If we cannot find them government may come after City of Mars. They may try to ban us. I am not allowing that to happen. If you don't say what you know, I am going to blow your head off." As she was about to draw her gun, Rico quickly moved her away.

Taz was a little shell shocked. How could she just slap an adult man? And the threat to blow his head off! This girl was total nuts. Her concern about the city sounded overblown. There was never an instance where a resort was banned for the action of others.

Before Ron could respond, a noisy commotion broke down at the entrance. Moments later, a bomb or something of that nature blew off part of the heavy metallic door. A few shadowy figures forced their way inside and started to shoot indiscreetly. Deadly laser rays rained down on every direction, looking for victims. Several guests were hit before they even realized what was going on. Terrified ear piercing screams filled the air.

"They are here," Ron screeched. "I knew it. I am dead. Rico, please save me. I know who did it."

"Who? Say it and I'll try to save you," Rico shouted.

There was another blast around the center of the main hall room. A full scale battle was in progress now with both parties shooting back and forth. The hall room was filled with heavy smoke that was quickly spreading. Laboring to see through, they vaguely saw a group of tall men approaching them. Pete, Michelle, and Jason quickly drew their guns. Mila already had hers out and was ready to go berserk.

"Take the Exit," Rico instructed. He grabbed Ron and made his way out of the exit to the alley at the back. Rest of the team stayed right behind him. The advancing intruders had not yet taken any shot at them.

"We won't shoot unless they shoot," Pete said. Michelle, Jason and he surrounded Larisa, Jing Jing and Taz.

Taz thought his heart was going to jump out of his chest. He kind of knew there was a remote possibility of them being in a situation like this, but he never thought that would become a reality so soon. Larisa and Jing Jing looked less nervous, giving an impression that this wasn't their first time in a situation like this. "Don't be afraid," Larisa whispered to him. "Those three are great fighters."

Mila was at the front of the group holding her ten inch high beam gun with both hands, ready to shoot. She looked fearless, determined. Rico stayed right behind her with Ron glued to him. They hurried through the alley, took couple of turns to come to a connecting road. Looking back, they didn't see anybody come chasing at them. Rico connected to his Limousine and instructed it to use auto drive to come get them. "It will be here in thirty seconds," he said.

Right at that moment, another loud blast took place very close to them. The ground shook heavily as if an earthquake was in effect. A black car with tinted glass zoomed in and screeched to a hard stop very close to them. Three tall, skinny men jumped out of the car, all armed. "Give us Ron," One of them said in a calm, cold voice.

"I am not coming," Ron screamed. "I am not afraid of the devil Wolf."

"Wolf?" Rico was surprised. "Which Wolf? Dark Wolf?"

Before Ron had a chance to say anything, a deadly laser came rushing and pierced through him. None of them noticed when a fourth man had approached them on foot and taken Ron down. Mila took less than a second to react. With a quick turn and press she baked the killer. Pete knew they had to react. The situation could quickly become deadly. He pointed his gun at the three men. "Why did he do that?" He demanded.

Mila turned his gun at the three. "Just shoot them," She shouted.

There were hundreds of people around within a blocks distance. The blast had already caused some panic on the streets. If a laser fight broke down that could end up hurting lot of innocent bystanders.

"Not here," Pete said.

The three men quickly backed off and climbed into the car, which zoomed away, took a sharp turn, and was out of their views. Rico's limousine rushed in and stopped ahead of them. "Pete, I am going to chase them," Rico said. "Do you guys want to come?"

"Of course! We are all coming," Pete said.

They got into the car fast. Rico drove. Pete sat at the front. Mila huddled with the rest at the back. She was restless, excited. She frequently glanced out of the windows, looking for the black car with three men. Michele and Jason sat with their backs straight, looked alert. Larisa, Jing Jing and Taz sat quietly with their hearts pounding wildly. Larisa managed to smile, Jing Jing looked grave serious while Taz looked dazed, working hard not to show his fear.

Rico drove as fast as he could. The roads were crowded. He weaved through the slow moving traffic and was going much faster than the posted speed limit. He was able to detect the black car, which pulled in highway Zero. Rico went after it. Both cars zoomed ahead in deadly speed.

"The highway is not that long," Pete said. "Where do they plan to go?"

"Don't know," Rico said, accelerating further. "Incidents like this barely happen here. Couple of years ago our Smartmans had chased and captured a deranged man.

The guy went around and around on highway Zero for several hours. At some point his car ran out of gas forcing him to stop. But these three does not look deranged to me. They are professionals and unfortunately Smartmans. That's what is worrying me. I am afraid of them. They have no weakness, no conscience – unlike humans."

"Roni mentioned of somebody named Wolf. Who is he?"

"If he was talking about Dark Wolf, then he is a total menace. Complete rogue. He has a spaceship of his own. Nobody really knows exact nature of his business. Nowadays plenty of spaceships travel within our solar system. Many of them carry tourists and minerals from and to Earth. It is a general perception here that he robs those spaceships. He is like a modern day space pirate. Sounds fanciful, but actually disgusting. Giving us all a bad name. People on Earth think we are hosting them, willingly or not. Anyway, I didn't think kidnapping was his thing though. I am surprised."

"I have never even heard of him," Pete said.

"Clever guy. Keeps a very low profile. In last ten years he probably robbed four spaceships, to our knowledge. I doubt if all of the incidents got reported. We tried to find him. Had no luck. We don't even know where his hangout is. When he is not robbing he is invisible. Probably that's why he hasn't attracted much attention from the authorities on Earth. Until now, even Gary was ready to ignore the guy. But this time he went too far. And that's why we asked for your help. It was the last thing in Gary's mind. BSD services are not cheap."

The black car suddenly dashed out of the highway into a side road. Rico followed it but lost it soon after it made several quick turns and disappeared.

"Don't worry. I have tagged the car. We'll find them."

"Don't you want to call for backup?"

"They are coming. I already sent a request to our central security system. I think Gary himself is coming. He does not like any trouble in the city."

Rico turned several times as directed by the tag system but there was no sign of the other car. He drove around for a little longer in vain. "Damn! The stupid tagging didn't help at all," He said bitterly. "They must have found a way to cancel out the tagging mechanism."

His phone rang. Rico answered. "I lost them, Gary. They disappeared like ghosts."

He listened to Gary quietly. Disconnected.

"Those goons somehow got out of the city," He said, annoyed. "A private porter flew out of the city just minutes ago. Gary tagged it. Let's see if it works this time."

After turning into another connecting road, they found the black car, abandoned on the roadside. It had no number plates. Rico called up the central security system, gave the location of the car and asked to have it processed for evidences.

"They had a second car waiting," Pete said. "How far is the nearest porter landing?"

"A kilometer," Rico said, still unhappy. "They came fully prepared. I should have known better. We'll find them. Just matter of time. One thing I can't figure out is, why kill Ron? Even if he knew it was Wolf who took those tourists, so what? He must have taken them for a reason. He'll have to come up with some sort of demand, I guess."

"Perhaps it's not about Ron," Pete said. "He is just making a statement. Take me seriously. I mean business."

"May be. But he has never killed anybody before."

Rico drove the limousine back toward the hotel. Pete was thoughtful. "I need to know more about this guy Wolf. What do you have?"

"Not a whole lot," Rico said. "I'll send you whatever I have. What should we do now?"

"Nothing much, really," Pete said. "Let's find out where the porter goes. Hoping the tag would work. We'll have to plan accordingly. But I think you are right. He must have something in his mind. If we wait long enough, he'll come to us."

"Let's see what that bad ass has in his mind," Rico muttered.

# Chapter 8

After returning to the hotel everybody went back to their respective rooms. They were tired and needed a good shower, a quick meal, and a short nap to freshen up. Mila went home with Rico. He would return after a few hours.

Back to his room Pete called up CI-6 first and gave him a quick update. It would send a report to Dan based on Pete's update. Pete skipped the shower and sat at the computer. He needed to go through all the information that Rico had sent. He also called up Michelle and asked her to join him when she got an opportunity.

Michele took a quick shower, skipped the meal and showed up at Pete's room in twenty minutes. Jason had ordered some food for two of them, but Michelle turned him down. She was dying to know more about Wolf. Jason understood her eagerness, but didn't appreciate the rejection. He couldn't help himself but feel a little depressed. Instead of dining alone, he took the food and joined the three youngsters in Larisa's room. Jason was the last person they were expecting. He and Michelle always ate together. Jason didn't look like to be in his best mood. They decided not to bring it up.

Pete was surprised to see Michele show up so soon. "Have you eaten?"

"Not hungry." Michele said, standing at the door. "What did you get? Who is this Wolf? Does Dan know anything? What about CI-6?"

Pete chuckled. "You are never going to change. I asked you to come when you get a chance, not to leave everything and rush here."

"Are you going to let me in or not? I can't rest until I know everything there is to know about this guy."

Pete moved out of the door letting her in. She closed the door behind.

"I don't want to release all the information to the team yet," Pete said. "We have trainees in the team. We don't want to scare them."

"What have you learned so far?" Michele asked as she eased into a chair.

Pete pointed at the food on the table. "Do you mind sharing with me?"

"No appetite. Tell me what you know."

Pete ordered a pizza. He took a bite on a large piece and projected some information on the wall. "Rico sent me some information. Dan just sent something. Haven't received anything from the Controller yet. You are looking at the summarized version."

Michelle browsed through it.

For the last several years a spaceship named Dark Wolf had been getting some attention in some media on Earth. However, surprisingly there was very little information about the captain of the ship. There was an assumption that many years ago he might have gone to space with a company as a scientist to do some research work. He probably never returned to earth after that. It was thought that the spaceship Dark Wolf was built using the structure of another spaceship. Almost a decade ago, a cargo carrying spaceship was abandoned by the owners on Mars after it was damaged in a minor accident. A mysterious group quickly purchased that ship. Since then nobody had seen it again. It was assumed that the ship was modified and transformed into the current day Dark Wolf, which was powerful and equipped with modern instruments. In the last decade, all the piracies – a dozen or so - that were committed in the space near Mars were all blamed on Dark Wolf. In each of those cases primarily fuel was stolen. Even though nobody had ever seen the Captain of that mysterious ship, it was thought that the ship was named after him. There were no complaints ever filed against him on Earth due to lack of evidence. Hence, he had no known criminal records anywhere on Earth. He was not on the wanted list of any government. There was never a formal inquiry or investigation about him.

The document concluded here.

"That's all! Not what I was hoping for," Michelle said, disappointedly.

"I agree, not much," Pete shrugged. "But not very little either. At least we now know that there is some information floating about him on Earth. Not very useful information, but still better than nothing. We know almost nothing about the captain, but have some idea about the ship. It is an old model ship. Some work was done on it to modernize it. I doubt if they were able to do very much. Outside Earth how many large scale facilities are there to repair a spaceship? None."

"Don't be so sure about it. There are several companies here who are working on spaceship repairing and rocket engine development. But why are you concerned about his ship?"

There was a knock on the door. Michele opened it. She must have expected Jason but found Rico instead.

"We have news, Pete," Rico said.

"You know where the porter has landed," Pete guessed.

"Correct. Quite far though. About 1600 kilometers (1000 miles) away from here, there is a small resort. It is known to offer tourists illegal drugs and other activities. There had never been any complaints, so nobody cared.

That's where the porter went."

"I think I know what is going on in your mind," Pete said, smiling.

"What do you think?" Rico's eyes were bright in excitement.

Pete thought for a moment. "We don't have much choice."

"My point," Rico said. "If we want to attack, this is the right time. If we wait too long, he might suspect something and run away in the space. Where are we going to look for him there?"

"Agreed," Pete nodded. "Michelle, call Jason. Only three of us would go. Trainees can stay in the hotel. They have not received enough lessons to go in a mission like this."

Michelle shrugged. "It would be hard to explain that to them, especially Larisa."

"Try. If they are desperate then we'll see."

Michelle left quickly. Rico projected a map on the wall and started to draw lines on it with an electronic pen, describing the location and geological details of the target to Pete.

Twenty minutes later all six of them merrily climbed into the all familiar limousine. None of the trainees would agree to stay behind. Pete could insist but he decided not to. One of the main reasons for such trainee programs was to give them real time experience. This mission was relatively risky, he realized, but felt the risk wasn't overwhelming, not when Rico and his army of Smartmans were leading the operation. Still, he was responsible for their safety and having them with him meant much higher responsibility. His primary objective would shift from apprehending Wolf to keep the trainees safe. He was hoping with a little luck both would be achieved.

Rico drove fast to arrive at the nearest porter landing. They hurried into a waiting porter and were up in the sky in minutes. Despite their small size porters flew quite fast – no less than 800 kilometers (500 miles) per hour. They had two rows of seats that could accommodate eight passengers nicely. The pilot's cockpit was small, packed but good enough for Smartman pilots, who didn't suffer from claustrophobia. Their pilot, a hard faced tight lipped Smartman didn't even bother to welcome them or announce anything before taking off and rushing ahead at the top speed. It was Rico who informed them that it would take couple of hours to reach their target.

Rico projected a holographic image of the destination and started to provide everybody some details about the place. He had never been to the location, but was able to come up with a map by examining the satellite views and collecting information from people who had visited it. He believed it was a small resort with an area of thirty to forty acres. The resort was estimated to be five hundred feet wide and close to a mile in length. Unlike City of Mars, it was under one opaque roof, about hundred feet high. It had a single street that was located at the middle and ran lengthwise. All the stores, casinos, and hotels were located on both sides of this street. The resort had two external porter landings, one on each side. There were heavily built entrances every hundred meters, guarded around the clock. The resort had three layers – the outermost shell with the main entrances, a buffer zone accessible by another set of doors, and finally the oval central core separated by a thick, extremely strong wall where all the guests stayed, played, smoked, took drugs, and shopped. The outer two shells were more like safety zones, providing enough room for the armed security guards to secure the important central core.

"I think the entrances close to the landings would be most secured," Pete said. "Can this porter land on uneven ground?"

Rico shook his head. "It is possible but very risky. I wouldn't suggest that. A little miscalculation can cause serious accident."

"Where are we going to land?" Pete asked. "They

must be watching the landing ports."

"Tourists come here all the time. Do you think they would attack us before verifying our identity?"

"If Wolf is the one who kidnapped the tourists, and he is hiding there – yes, they just might shoot first," Pete said.

"Do you think we can beat them?" Jason asked. "We are only handful. They must have hundreds of guards."

Pete nodded thoughtfully. He was relying on the element of surprise to win this battle, but right now he was not very optimistic. This place looked well planned, well guarded. If Wolf was inside the resort with his cohorts – man or machine - it would be high risk to attack. He needed to decide quickly if they would go through the plan. Rico might have guided them here, but everybody knew it was Pete who needed to lead, because only he had the proper authority to intrude a resort. He also had three trainees to defend – not an easy task by any means.

Pete knew Rico didn't rush into this. He definitely had a plan, in the least additional gun hands. However, until now he hadn't given any hints of such backup force. Did it skip his mind or Pete was hoping for too much? Pete looked at Rico meaningfully. He had high hopes on Rico. This Smartman couldn't have underestimated somebody like Wolf.

"Don't worry," Rico assured him. "We came prepared. There are four other porters following us. Each of them is carrying ten Smartmans – total forty of them. They'll be at the forefront, leading the attack. We'll only move in when they have secured the place. I have no intention to put your team on harm's way."

"What is your plan?" Pete asked.

"Once we get close to the resort, we'll wait at a distance while our army of Smartmans attacks," Rico said. "I don't think he would expect such quick response. We should have an upper hand. He might try to escape. We'll have to stop him."

"How can you be so sure that Wolf is there?" Jason asked.

"Let's say, my sixth sense," Rico was serious.

"You are kidding, right?" Larisa curiously said.

"No, not really," Rico said. "It is possible to figure out a lot of things just by considering probability. And I do have a very advance artificial brain. I can calculate very fast. It's my strong feeling that Wolf is there, but not the hostages."

"Where does he keep his spaceship?" Jing Jing asked, breaking his long silence.

"In the space," Rico said. "Most probably on the Martian orbit. I believe he lives in the spaceship, coming down only when he needs something. He probably uses small probes or capsules to come to Mars because his spaceship never lands. If it did, we would know."

"I checked with head office on Earth," Pete said. "They do not have a whole lot of information about him. Have you ever seen him?"

"Nope. Nobody have. He wears a wolf-mask all the time. Who knows why?" He sent everybody an image of Wolf with his mask on. "One tourist secretly took this image. Normally all cameras are banned in that resort."

It was a full body image. He was at least six feet and several inches tall, well built, wrestler like body with strong jaws, wearing the unmistakable mask of a blue faced wolf with red and white stripes. It covered his face completely with only a pair of sharp eyes visible through the eye shaped holes on the mask. He had a fitting trouser and a turtle neck T-shirt on. "Wow! He looks cool," Taz spontaneously said, not realizing the impact of it.

Michelle chuckled. Who could blame a fourteen year old finding a masked giant fascinating.

"What?" Jing Jing mildly objected. "He is just a thug."

"Kind of cool," Larisa came to Taz`s rescue. "Why does he wear a mask though? Camouflage? Facial deformity?"

"No idea," Rico said. "There are all kinds of weirdoes in this space. But I think it's camouflage. No face, no identity."

"Isn't Mila coming with us?" Michelle asked.

"I hope not," Rico said. "I didn't ask her. She can be a big trouble. City of Mars is too dear to her, just as it to her dad. If she senses any threat against the city, she simply loses her mind. Right now, I don't think she is very happy with Wolf. Who knows what she would do? I didn't want to take any chances."

"You are scared of her, aren't you?" Taz said, jokingly.

"You should be too. Stay as far from her as you can. She is one tough crazy nut."

Larisa laughed out loud and gave Taz a meaningful nudge. Taz blushed. This girl had no sense of privacy. He winked at her several times, begging her to stop, but Larisa gleefully ignored. Even Michelle was grinning! Shame! Now everybody knew about his secret crash. How embarrassing!

# Chapter 9

The porter flew ahead zooming through the red, rough, and rocky landscape of Mars. The four porters carrying soldier robots had caught up with them and were now following closely. As they closed on to the target, Rico asked the pilot to slow down and allow the soldiers to move ahead.

Pete quickly checked on his team. Behind the Mars cover they looked brave and composed. The cover was a must to explore out in the Mars. The amount of carbon dioxide was too high in the air and was not breathable. Each Cover had a mechanism within it that produced and supplied oxygen for up to twenty four hours. It was also somewhat effective against low gravity, sand storms, and low energy laser beams.

Michelle and Jason were quietly discussing something. They looked at Pete briefly before going back to their conversation. Jing Jing was consumed with his mathematical problems as usual. Larisa and Taz looked alert but in good spirits, watching around them with curiosity.

Pete gave each of the trainees a low power laser gun. He had got them from Rico. "I don't usually give trainees weapons but I am not very sure about today's operation," He explained. "Use them only for defense. They are low powered. People won't die, might get paralyzed for a little while. As for Smartmans, you'll have to target at certain points of their bodies to deactivate them. Any of you had any training on laser?"

"Jing Jing and I got some training," Larisa said while Jing Jing just nodded.

Taz shook his head. "I didn't but I can shoot, though my skill is not something to brag about."

"That will do," Pete said. "Don't be afraid. We'll be around."

"I am not scared at all," Taz tried to look brave.

"There's no shame in being afraid," Pete said. "Fear increases our survival aptitude, makes us tougher."

Rico waved to get his attention. "A quick update," He said. "We'll reach there in ten minutes. Our porter will stay about 20 kilometers away. The soldiers would attack the resort first. Once they have cleared the way, only then we'll move in."

The pilot slowed down even further. The four porters carrying soldiers passed them quickly. There was no sign of the resort anywhere, though they could see it on the screen that showed the image from a satellite. In the next few minutes the pilot slowed down the porter to a total halt. They tried to relax leaning back on the seats. Taz could feel his heart pounding. He had never been in an operation this risky. He tried to hide his fear. Pete, Jason, and Michelle looked composed. Larisa excited as ever. Jing Jing was quiet. He was probably a little afraid too.

Taz had no idea that things would happen so fast. Not even a few meager minutes had passed when their porter started to move again. "They are in," Rico said.

"How come there were no sounds of shooting?" Larisa asked.

"All laser guns," Rico said. "The chances of blasts are very low. That's why you heard nothing. Pilot, please move as fast as you can."

The porter picked up speed quickly. It went over a series of high mountains to a patch of flat land at the center of which stood a large structure – this was their target. The four combat porters had been shooting high powered laser beams at the gates constantly. Several large holes had already shown up on the outer shell. There were also some indications that the inner walls had sustained some damage as well. A few robot guards shot back every now and then in an apparent futile attempt to stop the attackers. They seemed to be lacking both on manpower and weaponry. Most interestingly, the dozens of porters that sat peacefully on the porter landings made no attempt to take off to defend the resort. There were no signs of activity there.

"They are confused. We surprised them," Rico said. "They didn't think we would be here so soon. Pilot, drop us please."

The pilot slowed down the porter and landed carefully. All of them climbed out in a blink, with their guns in their hands, ready to defend if attacked. They ducked and ran toward a collapsed wall behind Rico and Pete. A hundred feet of desperate running, fearing laser attacks from inside, finally ended when they safely slipped through the holes on the outer shell, created by the lasers, and entered the compound.

Right before getting inside, Taz almost intuitively looked up and thought he saw a porter zooming in from the direction of City of Mars. Unsure, he looked back a second time. This was when Rico saw it too. He didn't look happy. "That's Mila-the-big-trouble," Rico muttered unhappily. "I wish she would listen to me for once."

As they huddled into the inner shell, a few welcome shots were fired at them. Diving on the floor, they tried to slither away from the line of fire. Rico's soldiers had made their way into the compound as well. They shot several of the enemy robots and disabled them. Rico, on his feet now, ordered his soldiers to push deeper inside the compound and turned to Pete. "My guess is Wolf is hiding in one of the casinos. You should stay here with your team. My soldiers would take control of the resort in no time. Then we'll go look for him."

Rico left them behind and joined a group of his robots and went on to look for enemy guards. Pete asked his team members to stay low. They waited behind a few big pillars until the shootings stopped. Rico had taken the time to pop up and signal them to move ahead.

They came through the second layer of walls without any trouble and stepped into the oval lobby. Things got slightly challenging at this point. A group of resort guards had taken shelter behind steel barriers and were defending valiantly. Twenty of Rico's soldiers, who had entered the lobby earlier, diligently fought back. Rico and Pete skipped the battle and started to look around for an entrance to the center. Michelle and Jason took the trainees and stayed behind anything that looked strong enough to hold of runaway lasers.

"Why don't we join in the fight?" Larisa asked impatiently.

"We don't unless we have to," Michelle said. "We are investigators, not hired soldiers. We came here to solve a case. They are responsible for our safety."

Larisa nodded as if she truly understood everything Michelle said. The truth was her fingers were itching to get crazy with the laser gun Pete gave her. Taz noticed it.

"These guns are little better than toy guns," He warned. "Don't even think of fighting."

"Fighting against the Smartmans is easy," Larisa said. "You need to hit them on the central sensors. They have many sensors behind their eyes and neck. If you can hit a few of those sensors, they would turn into worthless piece of metal. I know I am not done with all my shooting classes, but I think I am good to go."

"Don't do anything stupid unless you are trying to get fried," Jing Jing teased. Larisa gave him a mock punch on the stomach, which was probably a little stronger than she intended because he gasped for air.

Rico and Pete were seen running up and down along the wall desperately looking for a way through. There were no doors, no windows, no magic buttons that opened up a secret door. Rico's robots had defeated the enemy guards and waited for next instructions. He asked them to shoot the wall down. Unfortunately, twenty laser guns hitting simultaneously had no impact whatsoever. Rico shook his head in despair. "Laser proof material. Very expensive. Most of the resort owners do not have the fund to buy this stuff."

"How are we going to enter?" Pete said.

"Wolf definitely knows we are here. Is he going to just sit tight?" Michelle said.

"Wolf may not do anything," Rico replied. "He must

have other ways to get out of here. May be a tunnel or an opening somewhere. If we want to catch him, we got to get in. But how? May be we should try the laser cannons. Let me ask them to bring the cannons. I doubt if this wall can stand against the cannons. One shot of cannon is as strong as ten thousand laser guns."

Pete looked a little cautious. "How safe is it? We don't know how many people are inside. I don't want any tourists to get hurt."

"Don't worry. These cannons are highly adjustable. We'll use them very carefully." Rico asked two of the Smartmans to get the cannons. They rushed out. Suddenly everything shook up, several times, almost like tremors of an earthquake. Before any of them had a chance to figure out what was going on, a section of the roof blew off and crashed down. Not sure what was happening, they all dived on the ground, covered their heads with their arms. "What was that?" Michelle shouted.

"Part of the roof just fell," Pete shouted back.

Looking up they could see several large holes in the middle of the roof with multiple cracks spreading quickly like bunch of snakes. With the roof breached, the oval wall that secured the core also gave up in areas. This was a good thing but they had little time to celebrate. The bombings continued with chunks of metals, concretes, and debris crashing down indiscriminately. They had to look for shelter.

"Who is bombing?" Pete asked moving away from the core.

"Take a wild guess!" Rico said with a strange mixture of annoyance and pride. "She is shooting cannons right from the porter. It got the job done though. Some parts of the oval wall opened up. Irresponsible but effective – I'll give her that. Going for that kind of destruction without even contacting us? Very irresponsible. She could have blown all of us away."

"She still can," Pete said. "Can you ask her to stop, please?"

"I am trying. She is too busy bombing. Not taking my calls," Rico muttered hopelessly. "She'll keep on it until there is charge in the cannon. Anyway, you guys stay here. I'll go in with my soldiers and look for Wolf."

"I am coming with you," Pete said. "I need to make sure the two hostages are safe."

Rico shrugged. "Your choice. Gary asked me to take you guys back in one piece. Come alone. There could be more guards inside. They may have stronger weapons."

Rico slipped through one of the openings in the oval wall and disappeared into the core followed by couple of dozens of his Smartmans. Pete signaled Michelle and Jason to stay in the lobby along with the trainees and followed

Rico. Just seconds after he disappeared inside the core, the roof shook up again with a load of debris flying to the ground. Several screams filled the air.

Michelle ran. "I heard Pete. He must be wounded."

Jason grabbed her hand. "You can't go there. It can be dangerous."

"Pete can be in trouble," Michele insisted. "You stay here. I am going to look for him."

"Pete can take care of himself. Don't go," Jason said.

"Jason, this is not the right time for jealousy," Michele snapped. "I am the assistant captain. I have a responsibility."

Jason looked shocked. "I am worried about you, that's all. Let me go. I can help him more."

Before Michelle could respond an automatic gun shot out hundreds of bullets. Each bullet burst as it struck any hard surface. They all hugged the ground.

"I had no idea these guns were still in use," Larisa said, surprised.

"They are not regular guns," Jing Jing said. "Each bullet bursts once it hits something hard and then throws lasers all around it. Very dangerous."

"That's why they are banned on Earth," Michelle said.

More shots were fired with deadly laser beams

dancing all around them. They crawled further back and took shelter behind a thick wall that was still intact. Michelle tried to contact Pete using her remote connector. The connector was designed to be able to find out local satellites and be able to connect with the target. When necessary, they were also equipped to penetrate firewalls. After several tries she finally got connected. "Pete! Pete!"

"We are in trouble," Pete almost whispered.

"Where are you?" Michelle asked wearily.

"Inside a casino," Pete said. "At first, it seemed like there was nobody around, but they were hiding. They attacked us may be a minute after we entered the core. Several of our robots have been deactivated. Rico is still fine. We are hiding right now. We are not sure how strong they really are."

"Is Rico with you?"

"No. I have been wounded a little. He left me here and went on to fight."

"What do you mean by wounded a little?" Michele panicked.

"Don't worry. It wasn't laser. A steel bar fell on my shoulder from the roof. One part of the shoulder became numb. I'll be okay. Stay where you are. I can still move both of my hands. I can still shoot."

"I am coming. I think I have a general idea about

your location." Michelle didn't allow Pete to object. She rushed ahead. Even Jason did not have a chance to stop her.

"Shouldn't we all go?" Larisa said.

"No. We'll just create more problems," Jason gloomily said. He could not hide her anxiety.

There was another explosion nearby. More rubble dropped from the roof. A small group of robot guards, who were running toward the exit, possibly trying to avoid the falling debris, spotted them. They paused, discussed briefly, and came running with their guns raised. Jason knew this was bad news and he had to do something quick. Sometimes attack was the best defense. He attacked first, with all his might. His gun started to blurt out laser rays like colorful flower petals. A trained and skilled marksman, he hit couple of the robots midway, making them collapse on the ground. The rest changed strategy and quickly hid behind the pillars and called for reinforcement. Within thirty seconds an army of dozen robots appeared.

"Where are all of our soldiers?" Taz panicked.

"They must be inside the core," Jing Jing said. "There seems to be a big battle going on there."

"Jason, do you think we have a chance against all of them?" Larisa looked alarmed.

"With warriors like you in our team, why do we need to worry?" Jing Jing quipped.

"This is not the time for jokes," Larisa shot back.

"Crawl back," Jason instructed. "Keep your heads down. Stay low. They might attack anytime. Hurry up."

They didn't have time to move too far back. The guards grouped up and attacked in unison. Facing a swarm of lasers coming their way they did the only thing that were left to do – ran as fast as they could along the oval wall, away from the guards. Jason continued to shoot back as they ran but hit barely anyone. The trainees had taken out their guns and were shooting in all directions. The guards readily knew their guns were little better than toys. They didn't care much.

"If we could somehow get out of here, one of our porters could pick us up," Jason said, running fast.

"There is a gate right ahead of us," Larisa shouted.

The gate was more than twenty yards away, behind a series of tall pillars. It was unguarded. The guards must have joined the rest to fight back the intruders.

"Do you think it's open?" Taz expected the worst.

"Let's hope so," Jason didn't slow down.

They ran as fast as they could. Larisa was falling behind. Taz grabbed her by the arm and pulled her with him. "Don't be afraid. I am with you."

"You better! Or I'll beat you up later," Larisa growled.

Taz couldn't stop the chuckle. He saw the army of robots

coming around the oval with their guns blazing. They turned to their right into a short hallway and ran to the gate at the end of it. It was exit only, allowing only way out. They burst out in the open. The Mars covers helped them breathe but nothing to handle the lack of gravity. Attempt to run only resulted in them rising high, somersaulting uncontrollably. The guards came out chasing them. The gravity showed no mercy to them either, but they cared little, and continued to shoot while comically trying gymnastic like maneuvers to retain balance. Jason was too busy slowing down so that he could stand on his feet and had little chance to shoot back. He realized if they didn't get some help very soon, they could end up getting roasted.

As if to answer his prayer, a porter zoomed in, dived like an eagle close to the ground and rained down bullets on the guards, blasting several into pieces. It flew back up, turned around and came rushing back so quickly that the rest of the guards had no time to retreat. They tried to fight back but had no chance against the rapid fire variable power cannons boarded on the wings. The pilot shot several others forcing the rest to run away.

"Must be Mila," Taz excitedly said.

The porter went back up again. When it returned it

flew much slowly, almost in a gliding speed. As it closed on they could see Mila in the pilot's cockpit.

"Mila!" Larisa raised both of her arms and waved.

# Chapter 10

Mila lowered the porter down to twenty feet to the ground and kept it still. She dropped a metal ladder and as soon as Jason and others grabbed a rung, pulled it up to the porter.

Once inside, they quickly took seats at the back and strapped in. There was no telling what Mila's next move would be. Another group of guards had streamed out of the same gate and readily knew what had just happened. Mila didn't wait. She turned and flew away to safe distance. Now, she turned her head and smirked. "Do you see what happens when you leave me behind?"

"It was Rico's idea," Taz was quick to clear him up. "We had nothing to do with it."

Mila rolled her eyes. "Who asked you?"

"Who did you ask?"

"Anybody else," Mila frowned. "Where are Pete and Rico?"

"In the core," Jason said. "Pete could be in some kind of danger. Michele went to help him. We are not sure exactly what is going on inside."

"Nothing to worry about," Mila said. "With Rico there, nothing bad would happen. Top robot. Only problem is – too bossy."

"Why don't we go help them?" Larisa asked.

"We'll go," Mila said. "Let Wolf kick his ass for little longer. You don't come without Mila."

She backed up further away from the resort, faced it and set the porter to still. "Let's enjoy the show," she said.

At a distance, they could see glimpses of the compounds inside the core through the collapsed roof. Clearly, a heavy battle was ongoing there. Laser beams ran back and forth, sometimes lonely ones, sometimes in groups. Taz, Larisa, and Jing Jing looked at each other. Rico and the soldiers probably could use some help. The five portals that had carried the robot soldiers were all parked in the portal landings and appeared to be waiting.

"Are we just going to sit here?" Larisa sounded impatient.

"That's the plan," Mila said with a straight face.

"We can't just go and start shooting," Jason said. "We could end up hurting our own guys. Rico would probably let us know when he needs help."

"Why don't we get in touch with him?" Jing Jing urged.

Mila giggled. "Oh no! I am not doing anything. If he needs help he must beg. Leaving me behind! How about now? Are your stupid robots going to save your robotic ass? Pardon my language." She giggled some more. "This time I

got him. Here is a lesson for you, good old Rico!
He…he…he…"

Michele slipped through the opening in the oval wall,
stepped inside the core compound and quickly ran behind a
series of stores that stood by the road. She waited for a few
seconds to understand the situation. Looking around she saw
no moving things – humans or robots. Determining it would
be safe, she slowly advanced toward the center of the
compound, keeping as low as possible. The main street that
went across the core was about half a mile long with rows of
buildings of various sizes and heights, mostly three-four
storied, lining up along it on both sides. Some of them had
large neon signs with the word **Hotel** on it. They were used
for guest housing. The compound was lit in bright white
light coming from sources set high in the roof, which with
some damages still looked pretty intact and strong. She
crawled further down and then tried to contact Pete again.
"Pete! Pete! Where are you?"

"Michele? Where are you?" Pete asked.

"I am inside the core," Michele said. "But I don't see
anybody. Why is it so quiet?"

"There was a round of fight just moments ago. We
lost a few soldiers. It'll start again. Wolf is here. Rico was
right."

"Where are you?"

"I came out through the back door of the Casino. The first building on the other side of the road. Don't try to cross the road now. They may be watching it."

"How are you feeling now?" Michele asked. "Do you think you can run out of there on your own?"

"I think so. But there's no strength on the right shoulder. I doubt if I'll be able to run fast. I want to wait a little longer."

"Where is Rico?"

"Somewhere around. I haven't seen him for a while now."

"I am coming. Wolf must know your identity by now. Who knows what he is going to do if he finds you. Just stay where you are."

"Be careful."

Michelle disconnected and crawled forward. She checked on both sides of the street but saw nobody. Everything had turned so quiet suddenly! She didn't like it at all. Where did Rico and all his soldiers hid? Where were Wolf and his men? As she came near the street, she lied down still for a few moments. It was at least forty five feet wide. If somebody was watching, there would be plenty of time to hit a target moving across. Should she wait or just run across the road? It was quite possible that if she bolted she would be able make it safely.

Just then started another round of gun fight. The blood red lasers danced around the compound, almost silently, filled the air with smoke from the burnt objects. Watching the directions of the lasers, she knew most of the fight was happening at the other end of the compound, several hundred feet away from where she was. She didn't wait any longer. Keeping her head low, she ran across the street, cleared it and dived on the ground. No laser rays were shot at her direction. She doubted if anybody even noticed her. Keeping behind a series of stores located next to the sidewalk, she moved further west. There was no sign of any guards or guests anywhere. The fight had stopped again. The silence had come back. As she ventured ahead another hundred feet, she could finally see Pete lying down on the ground behind a large building. Pete looked both worried and relieved at her presence.

"I can't figure out what is going on there," he said.

Michelle checked his shoulder. Mars cover was intact. Good news. She pressed on the shoulder a few times and let go a sigh of relief. "Not as bad as I feared. It would heal within a few days. There's not much you can do here. Why don't we get out?"

"How about Rico? He might need help," Pete sounded unsure.

"We have no way to know where he is. From the lasers what I figured out, both parties are further down to the west. Rico must be there as well. There are no tourists here. Clearly Wolf was expecting us. Right now it appears to be deadlocked. We should leave."

"But I don't feel good leaving Rico behind."

"Rico is a robot. If anything happens to him he could be remanufactured. You are not a robot. On the other hand, he has his army with him. He'll be okay. You can't really help him in this condition. Can you even move your right arm?"

Pete could, but not very comfortably. It felt really heavy. "Where are Jason and the trainees?"

"I left them near one of the gates. Jason would know what to do," Michelle said.

Pete stood up on his feet. His shoulders felt stiff especially the right side. He even had trouble grabbing the laser gun with his right hand. He moved the gun on his left, so if necessary he would be able to shoot though not very accurately.

"Will you be able to run?" Michelle asked.

"I'll have to," Pete said. "Walking won't be an option if we want to get out of here alive."

"That's the right spirit!" Michelle teased. "Do you know how I felt when I heard you scream?"

"Joy?" Pete said, jokingly.

Michelle smacked him on the head. "Very funny!"

They checked around carefully before heading back to the gates. Michelle stayed at the front with Pete closely following. A slow smile hung between his lips for a little while before disappearing. "You do know Jason is jealous of me. I don't want to come between you two."

Michelle stopped and looked Pete into the eyes. "Jason has his place and you have yours."

"Where is that?"

"Where is what?"

"My place?"

"Do you want to discuss that standing here? Now?"

"That wouldn't be too bad. We might get a little smoked…"

"Just walk. And be quiet." They walked back the same way Michelle had come and stopped as they neared the edge of the street. Michelle had crawled ahead to take a peek when another round of fight broke out. It was short, no more than ten fifteen seconds. A lot of lasers were shot back and forth with no damages, at least nothing that Michelle could see from that distance.

There was a long, total silence – five seconds, ten seconds…What was going on, wondered Michelle. How was this going to end? They weren't hitting anything, neither were they retreating.

"Wolf! Wolf!" Rico's deep, powerful voice broke the silence. "I know you are here. Do you hear me?"

There was silence for several seconds. Then a strong, loud voice shouted back. "Rico! Rico! Rico! The robot who wants to be a human. I knew you would come to look for me. My dear friend, consider one simple point. You have no place to go. You are my prisoner now. I suggest you surrender peacefully."

Rico made his voice heavier, possibly to create a better effect. "Don't bullshit me. My men are surrounding this compound. You have no way to get out of here. Surrender, return the tourists, and I promise I'll not kill you. Pete might want to take you to Earth to stand trial but that is his problem. Once I hand you over to him, my work is done."

Wolf laughed in slow long stretches. "Don't forget Rico, this is my town. I knew very well that a foolish robot like you would look for any opportunities to attack it. If I want to get out of here, nobody can stop me."

"Is that so? In that case, please explain to me big shot, why you are still here?"

"I had this burning desire to play a little game with my robot friend. How about we do this? Forget all this laser-taser crap. Let's fight like man to man. What do you say? Or should I say, man to robot?"

Rico was quiet for a moment. He was thinking.

"Should he go for it?" Michelle asked.

"No, but he will. He is trying to get Wolf out in the open at any cost."

"Is he any match for Wolf? How strong are these robots?"

"Very strong. More than regular humans. I think in physical strength two of them are more or less equal. But Wolf can be a master of free hand combat. Not sure if Rico had such training. But he is an intelligent robot, best among all robots. He won't do anything foolishly."

Pete had barely finished, when Rico spoke out. "Okay. Ask your Smartmans to throw away their guns first."

"There's no need for that. I come out, you come out, we fight. I lose, the tourists are yours, and I stand trial. You lose. I get Pete."

Michelle startled. "What? Did I hear it right? Why is he asking for you?"

Pete shrugged. "Only god knows. I didn't even know he knew me."

"Don't be silly. You had been to Mars several times before. You are a famous guy. He must know you very well. Now the question is what does he need you for?"

Pete shrugged helplessly. This was an unexpected development.

"Okay," Rico replied back after a long pause. "But how would I know that you'll keep your word?"

"Why, you don't believe me?" Wolf chuckled. "Come out, Mr. Rico. Why such distrust? Are you afraid? You are a robot. What are you so afraid of?"

Rico had to make up his mind quickly. "Alright. I am coming out. Remember, if you betray me, there's no place where you can hide."

"Whatever you say. I am walking out, totally unarmed," Wolf said.

Lying low on the ground, Michelle and Pete stayed still, their eyes trained at the far end. A big man walked out of a casino with both of his hands raised above his head. He was over six feet tall. Under his skintight dress he had a well built body, like a wrestler. With a mask of wolf on his face, he looked quite strange.

Rico stepped out from a building on the opposite side of the street. He also raised his hands to show that he was unarmed. Both walked in short steps and stopped at the middle of the street, face to face. In size and shape both looked about the same.

"I don't get the mask thing," Michelle said.

"There are all kinds of nuts in this world," Pete shrugged.

Wolf didn't allow Rico any time to prepare and went

right into the attack. Rico predicted something like it and quickly moved out of his way. He had already figured out it would be a bad idea to get too close to Wolf. However, Wolf did not let him rest. He kept onto his aggressive tactics and continued to attack. Rico remained calm, but very cautious. He had no knowledge about Wolf's fighting abilities and he needed time to learn. The more Wolf attacked the better it was, as it gave him opportunity to gather more information. However, he needed to ensure that he didn't get damaged in the process. He had several weak points in his body. He knew about them and surely Wolf did too.

"Why isn't he attacking back?" Michelle was surprised. "He must be stronger than Wolf."

"Just being stronger is not good enough," Pete said. "Robot's do not yet have flexible bodies like us. Looking at the way Wolf is attacking, he is definitely expert martial artist. It would be difficult to beat him by using only strength. I have seen in my own eyes a five feet tall Chinese karate master defeating a robot of Rico's size and strength in about thirty seconds."

# Chapter 11

Pete had hardly finished the sentence when Wolf did something unexpected. He charged at Rico but Instead of attacking with his fists, he suddenly did a front handspring and hit Rico right on the chest. Rico was caught slightly surprised. He tried to move away but Wolf was quick and had adjusted his direction on the flight as well. The kick was strong and shook Rico on his feet. He stumbled back several steps and fell on the ground. He sprung back on his feet expecting another attack. Wolf used the momentum in full. He charged again but at the last moment dropped on his side and slid ahead hitting Rico on his tibias. Rico collapsed on the ground heavily. He tried to roll away but Wolf jumped in the air like a tiger, pinned Rico under his body and grabbed his neck with his hand. The neck was an important part of Rico. It connected between his head and body with a thin thread like stuff protected by a layer of thick, flexible material. Any damage to the thread could practically kill Rico. Pete knew right away Wolf had the strength to break Rico's neck in one jerk.

"What's now?" Wolf said. "Where is Pete? Call him. Once I have Pete I'll let you go. I'll even return your tourists. I have nothing against you. Do you get it, Mr. Robot?"

"There is no question of handing over Pete to you," Rico said bluntly. "He is a government employee. His job is to throw criminals like you in jail."

"I see! So you want to break your promises?" Wolf bitterly said. "In that case I have no option but to end your robot life first, and then go and look for Pete myself. Where is he going to go anyway? Must be hanging around somewhere."

"You won't be able to go too far," Rico said. "If anything happens to Pete, the whole department will come after you. They will chase you around like a rat."

"Good bye Mr. Robot!" Wolf was about to increase the pressure on Rico's neck, when he caught some movement at the other end of the street by the corner of his eyes. He stopped and looked up.

Without giving Michelle any opportunity to stop him, Pete stepped out in the open. Michelle was about to follow him but Pete calmly said, "Don't."

She hesitated for a few moments. Wolf didn't know about her presence yet. It wasn't a good idea to show herself. That could actually put Pete even more under pressure. She sighed. Knowing Pete, she should have realized that he would never desert a friend. The risk was too high, but Pete definitely was fully aware of that. Under normal circumstances Michelle wouldn't worry. He was highly skilled

Martial artist. He could deal with any fighter let alone Wolf. The problem was – he wasn't in best of physical conditions. With a damaged shoulder and a frozen hand it would be practically impossible for him to face a strong and skilled opponent like Wolf. She was terrified. She must find a way to save Pete without revealing her presence. But the question was, how? Where did Mila go? She could probably help right now. Or could she? Indiscrete bombings could possibly do more harm than good.

As Pete walked toward him with a slight limp, Wolf let Rico free and stepped back a few steps. It wasn't difficult to see the lines of smile that became prominent under his mask. Rico jumped out of the ground and walked briskly toward Pete. "Go away, Pete. I'll take care of him. Boss ordered me to make sure no harm comes to you."

Pete signaled him to be quiet. "He has some kind of plan. I am trying to find out what it is. Have you found out anything about the tourists?"

"Nope, I don't think they are here," Rico said. "They could be in the spaceship."

"Where does he keep his probe that he uses to fly back and forth to the spaceship?"

"Don't know. I couldn't find it. But it appeared that they were expecting us."

"What's the matter?" Wolf impatiently said. "What is

that love talk going on there? Pete! If you are brave enough, just come and fight me. These robots are good for nothing. Let's see how good the human babies from Earth are. Rico, move out. Let him come."

"That's what I thought too," Pete said to Rico. "This was a trap. Though, he probably didn't think we would attack with such might. Where is Mila? Didn't we see her flying this way?" Pete whispered as he walked past Rico.

"Must be up in the sky," Rico replied with his back to Wolf. "Should I get in touch with her?"

"Yes, she should connect with other pilots and coordinate an attack to allow your army to get out of here," Pete mumbled as he walked toward Wolf. "Also move Michelle and rest of my team to a safe distance. Michelle is hiding down the street."

"What about you? I can't leave you alone. Boss's order." Rico turned around. Pete had already gone past him.

"Don't worry about me," Pete muttered. "I'll tackle him somehow."

He was about fifty feet away from Wolf. With his muscular, big wrestler like stature coupled with the strange mask, Wolf looked quite intimidating. It was obvious he trained regularly and seemed to be at the top of his efficiency. Pete had very high level of confidence in his own abilities, but the wounded shoulder would be a problem. He could barely raise his right hand. Under normal condition he probably wouldn't have to worry too much about Wolf. He wasn't very young, that was obvious. Watching his skill and speed Pete assumed Wolf would be around forty five years old. He was strong, fast and acrobatic – a deadly combination. Robots like Rico, no matter how smart, were no match for him. Especially, not against somebody like Wolf who definitely knew how to beat a robot. He probably practiced against robots. Pete stopped when the distance between them was at thirty feet.

"Where are the tourists, Wolf?" Pete asked calmly. "You know who I am. It is my mission to get them back safely."

"Pete! Pete! Pete! Good to meet you finally," Wolf said.

"Can't say I share the same enthusiasm."

"I guess not," Wolf said, laughing in slow, long stretch.

"Tourists?"

"Let's fight on that. You win they are yours. I win you come with me. They go free. It's a win-win situation." Wolf chuckled.

"What do you need me for?" Pete tried to be calm. He knew he had to match Wolf's confidence.

"Everything in due time. Ready to fight?" Wolf took

a few steps ahead. "Must be the work of rubble?" He pointed at his wounded shoulder. "It must hurt. Can you move that arm? I am going to hurt you right there."

Wolf came rushing like a bull, leaped up in the air when ten feet away and tried to smash into him with his knees. He was faster than Pete expected. He sprung back on his one good hand and narrowly escaped the attack. Back on his feet, Wolf was surprised. Most fighters would become shaken faced with such forceful attack. Pete looked very composed and controlled, even with his one good arm. He knew this was not an opponent to be taken lightly. He advanced in small careful steps, trying to think and not rush.

Pete wasn't feeling very good. His bad shoulder was throbbing. It could use some medicine. He wondered how long he could stand against this bull of a man. He tried to relax and stay watchful. Over confidence could work against Wolf, forcing him into blunders.

Seeing how easily Pete avoided the first attack, Rico knew Wolf wasn't going to have a picnic. Even with his bad arm Pete could probably hold him off for some time. Little relieved, he contacted his soldiers, who were hiding in the casino and instructed them to head for the gates as soon as air attack started. Next he went to look for Michele. "Are you okay?"

"I am fine. Do you think Pete can handle him?"

Michelle looked pale.

"He'll be fine. For a while. I am calling in the pilots. Pete asked us to attack. Where are your team members?"

"Not sure. They were close to the gate. Ask Mila. She might know."

"Let's see if I can connect to her," Rico said.

He called Mila. No answer. Rico tried several times in vein.

Wolf did not want the fight to go on for too long. That would not only enhance Pete's confidence but may also make him (Wolf) tired. He was no more a young man and could not afford to chase around a twenty two year old man. Pete was a good fighter. One tiny mistake and Pete could get on top.

He attacked again. This time he came running with his feasts ready to strike but dropped on the ground and slid at the last moment with his feet looking to crash on Pete's lower legs, forcing him to collapse. This was one of his signature moves, very effective.

Pete knew Wolf was going to try something unexpected. He was a clever fighter. He (Pete) waited until Wolf came near him before somersaulting over Wolf, who slid past him. Wolf was back to his feet quickly. He was thoughtful, planning his next attack. Pete looked for Rico with the corner of his eyes. He couldn't see him. Rico was probably behind the building with Michelle, he assumed. Why wasn't he initiating the attack? Pete wasn't sure how long he could hold off Wolf.

Mila decided to ignore Rico's call. He deserved it for leaving her behind. But she still kept a keen eye into the dome through the holes created by the bombings. She didn't see much from that distance. It would be better to remain close, but that would have also made her porter an easy target for the guards. She sensed the impatience that was growing fast among the Space Detectives who were quietly sitting at the backseat. They are eager to get back into the battle. Mila ignored it. She hardly cared about other's opinion. She didn't even like most people. The boy was cute, she reluctantly thought, especially when he smiled. Since coming to Mars, she hadn't met too many kids of her age. Most tourists who came to visit were middle aged or older. Even when some young kids came, they were usually spoiled brats of rich people who acted as if they owned the planet. She could not tolerate those jerks. Was her father any less rich than anybody else on earth? He owned the City of Mars! Did she show off? May be a little, but she had every right to.

"Who called?" Jason asked.

"Rico," Mila briefly said.

"Other porters are flying to the compound," Larisa excitedly said. "Talk to Rico, Mila. He must have a plan."

"I have the same feeling," Taz cautiously added.

Mila had already noticed other five porters were advancing swiftly toward the dome. Were Rico and his party in danger? Did he call Mila because he needed her help? Probably. Waiting any longer could be disastrous. Shifting her weight in the seat, she spun the porter around its axis several times before following rest of the porters.

"Good girl!" Taz muttered.

"Be quiet!" Mila snapped. "Do you know I can beat the crap out of you?"

Larisa grinned as she nudged Taz hard on the side. Taz rolled his eyes. He had no desire to get Mila mad.

Rico called again. Mila received it this time. "What's the matter? Why are you bugging me? What do you want?"

"Wolf and Pete are fighting it out. Pete asked me to attack," Rico calmly said.

"Where should we attack? Do you want us to bomb on you?" Mila snapped.

"Bomb the roof. Do exactly what you were doing before. Our soldiers are stuck. Create a diversion, so that they can escape," Rico patiently said.

"Aren't there any tourists there?"

"None. They were prepared. It was a trap."

"Trap? For whom?"

"Pete."

"Pete!" everybody echoed.

"Why Pete?" Jason asked.

"Don't know," Rico said.

"Where is Michelle?" Jason asked anxiously.

"She is with me," Rico said.

"Have you informed dad?" Mila asked.

"No, not yet. Be careful. I don't trust Wolf." He disconnected.

Mila accelerated. Other Porters had already reached the compound and were hovering over it. They were probably waiting for Rico's order.

Wolf could not gain any advantage even after several attacks. Pete didn't even try to hit him. He kept on moving out of his way. Wolf was getting a little mad. He knew it wouldn't be easy, but had no idea it would be so difficult. He did not have a lot of time in hand. He needed to wrap this fight up. But how? He looked around searching for his guards. They were all positioned inside the buildings, ready to shoot. The problem was Rico's soldiers were prepared to fight too. There was no element of surprise. Looking up he saw several porters hovering above the damaged roof. Was Rico planning something? He connected to his robot guards and asked them to attack back with full force, if attacked.

"You look little scared, Mr. Wolf," Pete joked.

"You are much more skilled than what I had guessed, I admit," Wolf said, smiled dryly. "But you are still not good enough to stand against me."

"You are not going to win this fight with big words. I say, just surrender. You aren't going to get a long sentence for just the kidnapping. May be twenty years, could be less, if you hand over the hostages to me."

"Don't give me false hope. I was really starting to like this little fight but I don't have much time in hand. This game needs to end here." Wolf took a knife out of his garment and threw it at Pete with a quick jerk of his hand. Pete allowed it to zip by him leaning away from it. "Why try such childish move?"

Before he had finished, Wolf threw several more knives at his direction. Pete rolled on the ground twice and moved to safety. Wolf wasn't ready to give up. He charged again, this time with a flying kick, trying to hit Pete right on the chest. Pete did a backhand spring and went out of his reach. Desperate, Wolf followed him and tried to rain powerful blows at him. Pete saw an opportunity to hit back. Wolf came too fast, too close and wasn't fully balanced on his feet. Pete jumped up and threw a double kick right on his face. Wolf tried to move away, but was a little too slow.

Blood gushed out of his broken nose, streaming on the ground as he was thrown back on the ground. Embarrassed, Wolf hurried up to his feet and tried to wipe off the blood with his shirt. That's when another part of the roof burst into rubble. Broken pieces of metals, wires and other objects started to rain down on him.

After the first wave of attack, Wolf's army streamed out of hiding and counter attacked. Rico's soldiers had little choice but to face them. Soon another round of battle started, just more intense this time. Wolf took something out of his garments and smashed it on the ground. Within seconds a radius of fifty feet got filled with heavy putrid smoke. Pete held his breath and ran at him but couldn't see which way Wolf headed. Fearing Wolf might attack or he might get hit by one of the random laser rays that danced all around the place, Pete decided to play it safe. He dived on the ground and crawled away from there. Rico noticed him and came running. "Where is Wolf?"

"Gone. Where can he go?"

"No idea. If he tries to escape via ground, my guards will kill him. I suspect he'll try to fly."

Pete hesitated for a moment. He really didn't want to lose Wolf, but at the same time wasn't ready to take too much risk to catch him. If Wolf had any business with Pete, he would make sure the hostages were safe. Right now that was all Pete cared about. Pete had just taken out his gun, when two large panels in the roof silently opened up and a small probe zoomed through the gap leaving behind a blast of sound. The hovering porters had no chance of stopping it. Within seconds it disappeared in the space.

"Gone!" Rico said bitterly. "And we don't have the hostages."

"Now what?" Pete said, thoughtfully.

"We have to chase him. Let's go back to City of Mars, take Space Tiger and go after him. We have no other choice," Rico insisted.

Pete didn't want to rush into it. First, he needed to find his team members. He hoped they were unharmed. He walked along Michelle and Rico and stepped out of the core through an opening in the oval. Wolf's guards continued to battle Rico's army inside the compound. Pete wondered how long would the guards go on. Wolf didn't leave without giving them some directions. What was it? Unless they surrendered, Rico's guards couldn't stop either.

Mila saw the three coming out in the open. She landed her porter. Her passengers quickly jumped out of it. Jason ran to Michele, hugged and kissed her. She blushed and quickly moved away. Pete felt drained. His shoulder was swollen, stiff. He needed some serious rest. He climbed into Mila's porter and relaxed into the back seat. He wondered what was he going to report back to Dan and CI-6. They weren't going to be happy. This simply didn't go as planned.

Rico walked to the porter. "Should we go back now?"

"What about your robots there?" Pete asked. "Aren't they still fighting?"

"I am thinking of letting Wolf's guys go. They are of no use to me."

"How do you plan to do that?" Pete asked.

"I'll pledge. Hopefully they already had had enough. I want to go after that thug," Rico bitterly said.

"Let's go back to the city," Pete said. "I need some medicine."

After returning to the City of Mars, they ate a little and went to bed early in the evening. They had a horrible day and needed some good sleep to freshen up. Pete went to bed but could not sleep. His mind was stuck on the hostages. He had to rescue them. But how? Rico was able to drive away Wolf's guards, and had his soldiers look through every inch of the resort but saw no sign of the hostages. Wolf must have had kept them in his spaceship. Clearly, his objective was to capture Pete. The hostages were just baits. But why? He told everything to Dan who promised to look into it. Wrestling to calm his mind, Pete felt if he could discuss this with Michelle that might have helped him clear his mind. But then, he didn't want to create any misunderstanding between Michelle and Jason. Calling her to his room at that hour would be questionable. The discussion could wait until next morning.

At the break of dawn Pete was about to fall asleep, when Gary knocked on his door. "Sorry to bother you but I have very important news," He said apologetically.

"Wolf contacted," Pete made a guess.

"Yes, he wants to release the two hostages," Gary gravely said.

"In exchange he wants me," Pete knew it.

Gary nodded his head. "The exchange will happen in the space. Here are the coordinates." He held out a paper at Pete, who took it.

Looking at the coordinates, Pete was alarmed. It was 200 million kilometers (120 million miles) away. Five days trip. "How would we contact him?"

"Once you are close enough, he would contact."

Pete hid his feelings but deep inside he was worried. There got to be some kind of deep mystery around Wolf. Unfortunately, nobody knew much about him. He (Pete) won't have peace of mind until this mystery was solved. After Gary left, Pete woke his team up and asked them to get ready in an hour.

"Where are we heading?" Michelle asked.

"To the unknown," Pete said, dramatically.

# Chapter 12

Pete quickly dressed up and called Dan on Earth. Dan didn't expect his call so early in the morning. He was a little surprised. Pete had already sent a detailed report about all the events that had happened the night before. If there was any emergency or urgent matter, Pete customarily called Dan up to discuss.

Dan did not like Wolf's demand. "Have you spoken to CI-6?" He asked in unusually heavy voice. He loved to sleep and rarely got up this early in the morning.

"I sent him my report," Pete briefly said. "Haven't heard anything back yet."

"Let me find out," Dan said. "There is no question of you going there. It is nothing but a trap. You know that, don't you?"

"I don't think we have any other choice."

"Jumping into his trap is not an option. We know nothing about this guy Wolf. Why is he so interested in you? You can't go before we have some solid information on him. Let me dig into it first."

"Dan, let's not forget president's daughter and her husband are in his hand. If we are not there on time, who knows what he would end up doing. Do you want to risk that?"

"I know, I know, we must do something. But before sending you in a situation like this, I need to know that you'll be safe. Stay in the hotel. Let me talk to the controllers."

"I had something else to discuss," Pete quickly said before Dan disconnected. "If we end up going, I would like to leave the trainees behind. Even today's operation was too risky. None of us thought it would turn out like that."

"Don't always assume that Gary knows what he is doing," Dan said. "I read the report. This was pretty foolish. Thanks God, it ended in a good way. Could be quite different. They were waiting for you. Anyway, you have raised a very good point. Even if you want to take them along with you, we would need parental consent. We only have their consent up to Mars. Going another 200 million kilometers would take you to deeper space. I believe there are legal issues here that need to be tackled. Let me talk to CI-6. He would handle this."

Dan disconnected. He would have to race against time to find any information about Wolf. He doubted if he would be able to find anything new, but he still had to try. He really hated the idea to allow Pete to drift away so far in the space without knowing the true identity or intention of Wolf.

Michelle got dressed and was the first one to return. She didn't even try to hide her excitement. To her knowledge, nobody from Space Detectives had ever gone that deep in the space before. Pete knew her very well. They had worked together in several missions and he truly admired her for her courage and enthusiasm. It was not always easy to see past her striking beauty.

"When are we starting?" She tried to sound normal, in vein.

"Not too soon," Pete said. He knew Michelle wasn't going to be happy.

"Why?"

"Dan won't let us go until he has more information."

"Do we have any other choice?"

Pete shook his head. "I doubt. We have to go. Dan knows that."

"He is worried. I can't blame him. I don't like this hostage exchange plan either." Michelle looked worried, her excitement gone.

"Me neither. I don't want to get into a trap."

"What are you going to do?"

"Don't know. We'll have to come up with some kind of plan. Wolf seems to be a seasoned criminal. It won't be easy."

"One more thing – we would need additional

parental consent for the trainees if they are coming with us," Michelle said.

Michelle had her eyes on everything. Pete admired her even more for that. Having her with him in a mission boosted his level of confidence. He knew he could rely on her. "Dan is working on it."

"Did he find out anything else about Wolf?"

"Nope. That surprises me. How could Wolf remain so unknown? Isn't this supposed to be the information era? We don't even know his real identity."

"Whoever he may be, he has definitely gone a long way to capture you. What do you think he wants from you?"

"I'll ask him when I see him," Pete smiled. "I hope he doesn't beg for another fight. My shoulders are stiff. I'll need to put some medicine."

Michelle went to the bathroom and got some medicine. She took off Pete's shirt and rubbed the medicine on his shoulder. "It contains nano-technology. Within few hours it'll heal all the damaged tissues. You'll feel much better. If you had put it on last night, you would be all good by now."

"Don't be so nice to me. Somebody else might get jealous," Pete said, almost joking

Michelle chuckled. "I know, and I love it," she said.

"Jealousy is a sure sign of true love."

Michelle turned quiet. The reason wasn't obvious to Pete. They didn't talk as Michelle continued to rub the medicine on his shoulder. The phone rang. Call from Earth. It was CI-6 and Dan.

"We don't have much to share with you," Dan said unhappily. It was clear how much he hated this whole situation. The last thing he wanted was to send his best Captain and investigator into a mission like that. But he didn't have any other option. After all, it was the responsibility of his organization to try to rescue the hostages. It didn't help that the hostages were the American president's daughter and son-in-law.

"CI-6 spoke to the parents of the trainees," he said. "They want to talk to their kids first before deciding. If they do not permit, leave the trainees in Mars with Gary. Now, I am going to ask you again – do you really want to do this?"

Pete shrugged. "It's my job. I have to go."

Dan didn't say anything. He knew very well Pete would never back off. CI-6 took this opportunity to open his mouth. "Pete, we are trying to send another ship there, but it is going to take some time. Try to delay the exchange as much as you can."

"We have no way to contact him," Pete said. "If we are late, who knows what he would do."

"We can't take any chances," Michelle said. "He

might get nervous. We don't want him to hurt the hostages."

"This whole thing sucks!" Dan muttered. "Secret services, F.B.I., National Security – all are putting immense pressure on me, as if I kidnapped President's daughter. Anyway, use your best judgment. We need the hostages to be safe. Both of you know how important it is. America is our largest contributor. The president himself signs on the cheque. Do I need to say more?"

"Don't feel guilty, Dan," Pete said. "We'll be fine."

"I really hope so," Dan mumbled.

"So, there's nothing else you could find about Wolf?" Michelle asked, a little bitterly. She didn't try to hide her disappointment. How could a world full of people know nothing about this guy Wolf?

Dan did not reply. "We are trying," CI-6 calmly said. "One thing is obvious that he took a lot of effort to wipe out his past. We are searching all over the world. We'll find something soon."

That didn't sound very promising. There weren't a lot they could do to help. In situation like this, it was the Captain who needed to decide. It wouldn't be appropriate for Dan to direct Pete sitting on Earth. He knew Pete would do the right thing. He asked Pete to keep him informed around the clock before disconnecting.

Michelle wasn't happy. She checked the room to

make sure that there were no surveillance cameras anywhere. "Is everything okay in BSD?" She asked thoughtfully.

Pete pondered for a moment. He readily knew what Michelle was hinting at. Could Dan be compromised? It was very unlikely but not impossible. After all, he was a human too. Could someone find one of his weaknesses and use him? How about the controllers? Corrupting them would be next to impossible. He had no reason to believe that BSD was withholding information about Wolf. He shook his head. "There is no reason to doubt Dan."

They sensed the presence of others outside Pete's room. "Let them come in please," Pete asked Michelle, who opened the door.

Seeing Gary, Mila and Rico with the rest of his team Pete was a little surprised.

"Rico is going with you," Gary explained. "Mila is very motivated to ride in the Space Tiger. So she is going too." Gary looked helpless. Mila could be very stubborn, they had already known it.

Pete knew he couldn't refuse Gary. After all, he was their sponsor. Gary knew it too. Pete asked Taz, Larisa and Jing Jing to call up their respective parents and take necessary approvals if they wanted to come along in this mission.

For Larisa and Jing Jing things went very smoothly. They had been to a few other missions, though never that far. Taz's case was quite different. His parents went from shaken to nervous breakdown. They flooded him with questions and concerns. Where were they going? Why? What was the duration? What were the risks? Etc. Etc. Initially, Taz was not very sure whether he really wanted to go or not, but since Mila was coming all his hesitation evaporated. He insisted his parents for their approval. Finally, an hour later his parents gave in though not before they spoke to Pete. Taz felt very embarrassed. Pete must have seen that because he patted him on the shoulder as if to say, he understood.

It took almost an hour to complete the approval procedure. "Pete, when do you plan to start?" Gary asked. "What did Dan say?"

"It's my decision," Pete said.

"And?" All the eyes stopped on him.

"The earlier we can start the better," Pete said. "We don't want Wolf to change his mind and do something unexpected. We have so little knowledge about him that there is no way for us to predict his next move. But I need an hour to take care of a personal matter. All of you can go to the ship. I'll join you little later."

"I have already arranged for re-fuelling," Gary said.

Pete thanked him. Once everybody left, he locked the door of his room from inside and called his mother.

It was hard to estimate Sicily Baker's age. She

couldn't have been younger than fifty that much was understood, but her great looks and tight body was more than enough to shake most men regardless of their age. But people, who had seen her issue political speeches, knew it was wise not to get too taken with her external beauty. Her political opponents had figured it out very well in last twenty years. However, she did have a very strong support in the form of her father, Adam Baker – a long time senator of United States of America, who had always gone out of his way to ensure a strong foothold for his daughter.

Sicily had been living with her parents in their big mansion for last twenty years. After she divorced her first husband Robert Brown, Pete's father, she had moved with her parents. She never remarried. Unfortunately, her only child Pete Brown showed no interest in following their political inheritance. He had moved away from his mother at the age of fifteen and joined the flying academy. There he did so well that next he joined the BSD. Since he became the captain of Space Tiger he had been so busy that he couldn't even make time to come see his mother. At least that's the excuse he always came up with. Sicily knew it wasn't completely true. When Pete was still very young, his parents got divorced. Couple of years after the divorce Robert died in a car accident. He had excessive amount of alcohol in his blood. It was possible that Pete held his mother responsible for his father's untimely death. He had gone further and further away as he grew older. He did call sometimes, but his visits became increasingly rare. Sicily used to seek out for him before, but once she realized Pete didn't appreciate it, she stopped. However, she still called to greet on his birthday, his father's death anniversary, and things of that nature. Both of those events had passed this year. She was considerably surprised and equally worried with Pete's call. After all, she was a mother more than anything.

"Pete! Are you okay, son?"

"I am good, mom. How are you?"

"I am alright. I haven't seen you for a long time."

"Two years only," Pete chuckled.

"To a mother two years is long time," Sicily sighed quietly. Showing weakness to his son never had any impact on him. "When are you coming?"

"Don't know. I am in Mars now. Some idiot kidnapped president's step daughter. I am chasing him."

Sicily was quiet for a few moments. "Why did Dan send you to Mars again?" She had deep anxiety in her voice. "I'll get mad with him this time. Isn't there anybody more senior in his team than you?"

"What does seniority mean, mom? They are not as good as I am." Pete could not stop from showing a little bit of pride to his mother.

"You are just like your father. Too proud," Sicily muttered.

Pete chuckled. "Why are you pulling that poor fellow into this?"

"Sorry. How is your rescue work going?"

"A goon named Dark Wolf has kidnapped two persons and ran away into deep space. I am going after him. Before I start, just wanted to talk to you."

"This is the first time," Sicily muttered. "Will I be able to contact you?"

"I believe so. Not sure exactly what kind of situation we'll be in."

"Pete, you are not opening up to me," Sicily almost pleaded.

"Mom, the kidnapper wants to exchange the two hostages with me."

"What? Why?" Sicily panicked.

"Don't know. Our department has little information on him. Everything is very vague."

"This is not right. Why would Dan send you in a mission like this? I am going to scold him for this. Don't go there."

"Mom, you know I'll have to go. I am just wondering if you or dad had ever known anybody named Dark Wolf. He could be using a different name. Do you remember anything of that sort?"

"Are you wondering whether somebody is trying to get to you to take revenge against our family?"

"I don't know what to think. I am exploring every possibility."

Sicily was quiet for a few seconds. "I don't know if you are aware of this, but your father went to mars once, before you were born, to work for a resort there."

"What type of work?"

"I believe, as a technician. I can't clearly remember."

"More details would help."

"I'll dig deeper. The problem is your father liked secrecy. You could bomb him and he wouldn't still say a thing."

"As far as I know, he was an engineer. What was all that secrecy about?"

"You are asking me?" Sicily bitterly said. "I married him because I loved him. There was a reason I left him. You are my child, I can't say you everything. But I doubt he was involved in anything that would put his family in danger. I can't think of a reason why this man – Wolf, would come after you."

"Don't worry mom. I'll figure something out. If you find anything let me know right away. You could also connect with Dan."

Pete hung up before Sicily could say anything else. He needed to go. Everybody had already boarded the ship. He had a bad feeling deep inside him. He was somewhat afraid to take this young crew and subject them to such risk. Even with the consent of the parents, it was his job as a captain to ensure everybody's safety. There was no room for failure. He couldn't even think of losing anybody from his team.

# Chapter 13

Gary wanted to take the whole team in his limousine as they were heading to the dock. The car had enough room for all of them and some more. Rico usually did not drive. He only drove when Gary was in the car. Gary did not like bumpy rides and would get mad at the drivers. The robots could be machines but they did not like people getting mad at them. They could easily figure out how upset a man was by noticing the variance in his voice and facial expressions. Anyway, problem occurred with his loving daughter, as always. Instead of riding the limousine, she climbed into her flying car. She also lured the three youngsters, who followed her the moment they heard about the flying car. Within ten seconds Mila had disappeared taking along Larisa, Jing Jing, and Taz. Before leaving, she did take the time to bestow his father with the information that they would come to the dock in a little bit. If Gary knew his daughter at all, he had no doubt she won't show up in any less than an hour.

It took Gary about fifteen minutes to reach the dock. Since then he had been eagerly waiting for Mila to show up. No sign of her. This was exactly what he had feared. Mila was having another feat of stubbornness. His calls weren't being answered. Gary sighed and sat heavily on a chair. Being patient wasn't one of his virtues. Michelle and Jason went up to the cockpit. Rico stayed with Gary. He could easily figure out how upset Gary was. But even he knew getting tough on Mila would do no good. If Mila was unhappy she could simply pack up and go back to Earth. Gary wasn't going to let that happen. Mila was a motivation to him, a primary reason to continue with this extravagant 'City of Mars' project. Gary waited patiently. It wouldn't be another hour or so before Pete would show up. So, they had some time in hand.

Mila took the car about thirty feet above the street and sped ahead. She had the only flying car in the whole City of Mars. When she flew over the streets, everybody watched her in awe, specially the tourists. On earth, some flying cars had been in the market for a while, but the usage never picked up in the cities. The main issue was the extra complexity that came with managing the flying traffic. They were primarily used in the remote locations where not too many flying cars were around. Anyway, as Mila madly zoomed ahead, Taz felt a certain jolt of nervousness. He was sitting next to Mila at the front row – something that Larisa had forced him into doing. He was supposed to feel good, but in reality he was truly afraid. Her driving was scary to say the least and the only thing Taz could think was the car hitting something and turning into a mangled piece of metal with all of them in it. He wasn't looking forward to die on Mars.

Mila aimlessly drove over the city a few times. It was not a very big city, but the planning and building of it was almost perfect. The roads and houses were neatly built in a grid like pattern with nicely arranged stores, small clear lakes, residential houses, some forests, silvery creeks running through the city lengthwise – it was obvious that while designing it a keen eye was kept on all the details. As they flew over the entertainment district, she pointed at the night club where they had visited the day before. The front of the building bore the sign of a large collapse. They saw no movement inside. The owners must have gone into hiding.

"We have a very large gaming facility in this city," Mila announced proudly. "Dad originally made it for me, but now it is open for all. Let me take you there."

"Shouldn't we head for the Space Tiger?" Taz mumbled hesitantly. He wasn't particularly thrilled by the idea of Mila harassing him in front of the other two.

It was a bad idea after all. "Why are you always trying to be such a good boy?" Mila snapped. "What is the problem in checking out a few things on our way there? Do you think you are going to get some kind of reward for being a mama's boy?"

Larisa and Jing Jing grinned openly. Taz realized he wasn't going to get any help from either of them. He shrugged in despair and kept his mouth shut. Who knew how she would react next time. If they arrived late, either Pete or her father would definitely take it on her. It wasn't Taz's job to protect her.

The gaming facility was at the center of the city, near the entertainment district. It was located inside a big multi storied building. The whole structure was spinning around its own axis, gently. Such beautiful piece of architecture was rare, even on Earth. Mila turned abruptly, and landed in a blink. There was a parking spot reserved for her at the front of the building. She parked the car at the designated spot and jumped out of it. "Come on guys."

She was bossy, confident, showed no intention to care what any of her companions thought. Taz was worried, if not terrified. This girl was trouble.

As they entered the rotating building, they were truly amazed. It was quite extravagant – from design to workmanship to size and shape. Inside it, there were numerous gigantic rooms with sky high ceilings that held life size ships, rockets, submarines and saucers wired in with the latest holographic technology to create appropriate surroundings. Each floor consisted of at least a dozen or more of such game rooms. There were long lines of men, women and children of all ages in front of each of the game rooms. It was quite obvious that most of them were tourists.

"We won't have to wait in the line," Mila proudly said. "Which game do you want to play? Spaceship? Warship? Submarine? U.F.O? Pick any."

"Warship!" Larisa excitedly said. Taz was alarmed. He coughed a few times trying to get her attention, but had no luck. Did they really have time to play games, he wondered.

Jing Jing gave Larisa a good nudge. "Are you sure?"

"We may not be back on Mars ever again," Larisa said. "Why not try it out? Just for a little bit. Pete won't show up in at least an hour. Don't forget it takes time to talk to Earth."

"If Pete or Michele gets mad, I am going to blame it on you," Jing Jing said.

"Really?" Larisa made a fist and tried to punch Jing Jing mockingly, who jumped back.

"Why are you guys wasting time?" Mila barked. "Come on."

As Larisa and Jing Jing followed her, Taz had no choice but to stay with them. He couldn't deny the fact that all that extravagant stuff had him seriously interested as well. There were similar facilities on Earth, but they were too expensive for most people.

They followed Mila into a very big hall room. It was over three hundred feet in length, a hundred feet in width and about 60 feet in height. There was a real life gigantic warship located at the center of the room. This type of warship was still at use on earth. Mila walked past the long line of waiting patrons to the Smartman guard, who was at the entrance and ordered him to let them in. The guard obeyed her, no questions asked. They took an elevator and came up to the upper deck of the ship. It was clear that Mila had been on this deck many other times. She knew the inside of it like the back of her hand. She sent back the Smartman, who came along, and showed her three companions the way.

"Was it a good idea to cut in the line like that?" Taz muttered.

"What other choice we had?" Mila responded bitterly. "We don't have the whole day."

Taz didn't say anything but he was feeling guilty. Many of the people in the line seemed to have been waiting for a while. There were also some young children, waiting patiently.

Mila entered the Operations room, the tactical center of a warship. It was a specious room with large maps, multiple computer consoles, radar and sonar repeater displays, and a polar plot on a transparent plotting board. This was a familiar setting to them. The controls in a spaceship were somewhat different but still had some similarities.

"Easy game," Mila said. "We'll have to operate this ship virtually, of course. Once we press on the start button, the game room would convert into an ocean with high waves. I hope none of you have sea sickness. How about you?" She asked Taz.

"I…I don't think so. There's no need to worry about me," Taz tried to sound confident.

"I hope not," Mila muttered. She slammed the start button.

They didn't expect things to happen so quickly. In moments everything around them – people, walls, ceiling – all disappeared. Heavy fog enveloped the ship. There was water all around them. High waves slammed against the ship, making it swing like a pendulum. Standing just on their feet became a challenge.

"What do you want to do now?" Mila asked. "War? Storm? Whirlpool? Whatever you want. All of them are lots of fun."

"War!" Larisa excitedly said.

"My favorite, too," Mila brightened up.

Jing Jing and Taz exchanged looks. None of them was particularly excited, but did not want to be identified as cowards in front of these two girls. Without waiting for their assent, Mila pressed another button. Another moment had hardly passed when suddenly the ocean around them shuttered in deafening sound; the ship shook heavily with bombs dropping all around them.

"We have been attacked," Mila shouted. "We must fight. Don't just keep looking like fools. Stand before a panel, guys. The game is very simple. You'll figure it out quickly."

The ship swung side to side so heavily that it became hard to stand still. Taz had to move to keep his balance. He walked to a control panel and held on to the controller. Momentarily the rules and regulations of the game popped up in the bright screen in front of him. How to shoot, fire cannons, throw missiles etc. Enemy ships were all around them. There was no time to waste. It didn't take too long for them to get totally engaged in the game. After all, it was a question of life and death!

Finally, when they showed up at the dock, it was already two hours late. Gary and Pete were standing on the platform, discussing something. As Mil and her friends rushed in, Gary gave them a grave look. Pete tried to maintain a serious posture though for a moment Taz thought he saw a glimpse of smile at the corner of his (Pete's) lips. Did he really smile? He couldn't be sure. This was a horrible offense – what they did. What was the punishment for such a crime? It was a really bad idea to go with Mila. However, Mila, the ringleader, didn't seem to worry at all about anything.

"Sorry, we ran a little late," she said unapologetically. "When are we flying?" The question was thrown at Pete.

"The ship took off one hour ago. Where were you?" It was Gary who responded.

"I just took them to the gaming center for a quick visit," Mila explained. "They were so amazed, dad. You should have seen their faces. Are you mad or something?"

"No, I am not mad. That's not my spaceship. It's up to the Captain whether he would allow you in the ship or not."

Pete coughed to clear his throat. "You guys shouldn't have come so late. Discipline is very important. But because it was your first slip, I am overlooking it. Get in the ship quickly and get into your suits. The ship will depart soon."

Sensing that the delay wasn't caused by them, Mila abruptly changed her attitude. "We kind of knew there would be delays. I could just sense it." She was about to head toward the spaceship when Gary stopped her.

"Miss Mila!" Gary called out. "You caused some undue trouble at the center."

"Trouble? Me? No way. Who told you this? Rico?"

Mila was defensive.

"Rico is inside the spaceship. He knows nothing about it. I got updates from the center. First of all, you jumped the queue. Secondly, you stayed much longer than allocated time frame. When the Smartman pointed it out, you misbehaved with him. This is not acceptable. There were many tourists, who were waiting in line for the games. I do not expect such behavior from you."

Mila twisted her lips. "How can you believe those robots and not me? I am going inside."

"Come give me a kiss," Gary softly said. It was obvious he wasn't going to have a great time sending Mila in this expedition. But he definitely didn't have any choice. Mila hugged her father lightly and hurried to the elevator. Taz, Larisa, and Jing Jing quietly followed her. They were just happy that Pete took it so lightly.

Gary waited until they were out of their sight. Pete's smile returned. "Keep an eye on her," Gary said. "I have indulged her too much, I know. But I have no choice. If I get tough she threatens to return to Earth."

"Not to worry. She is a good fighter. A little reckless but with proper training could become a great warrior someday."

"Don't indulge her too much. She'll take full advantage. I am warning you well ahead. Not only she would create trouble, she would also corrupt others."

"I'll manage her. Now, tell me how we can resolve the issue with the expenses? Dan has already called me twice." There was a slight worry in Pete's voice. He checked his watch. It was getting late. If he didn't show up on time Wolf might end up doing something unexpected.

Gary looked thoughtful. "I didn't really expect my investors backing off like this. They called me up this morning and asked me to inform you of this change. Trust me, I knew nothing about it."

"Honestly Gary, I am not concerned about it. I just want this to work out. My mind is occupied on how to get the hostages safely out of Wolf's hand. I was hoping, Dan would call you up and make an arrangement."

"Well, things are little cold between us. You don't need to know all the details. The truth is I do not have full control of everything that happens here. Though from outside that's how it may look like. My investors live on Earth. They are the ones who govern most of the things that happen here. When I invited you here, I had full approval from them. But now that Wolf has flown out of the vicinity of Mars, they are thinking it is no more our responsibility to rescue the hostages. If BSD wants to rescue the president's daughter and her husband, then it should finance the mission. I have no say in it."

"What expenses are we talking here?" Pete asked.

"Fuel. Docking fee. Not for this time. Only if you dock here again. Because Mila is going with you, you'll have to come back to drop her. I won't charge you for that."

"Thank you. Can you do me a favor? Can you please call Dan up and explain this?"

Gary nodded reluctantly. "Okay. I'll do just that. After all, he sent you here because I had asked for you. He could have found a lame excuse to send somebody else."

"Great! I am relying on you. I have a much bigger problem to worry about. I don't yet have any clue how I am going to handle Wolf. Will you be able to provide some kind of backup, if I need it?"

"We don't have anything like Space Tiger. But we do have two rescue spaceships. None of them goes half as fast as yours. So, if we have to send any of them, it would take pretty long. Just remember that. Isn't Dan sending anybody else to help you?"

"We had to deplete our fleet due to reduced budget. I don't know if Dan has any spaceship handy to send. Anyway, I am heading to the bridge. I'll be in touch."

Pete quickly rode the elevator to the bridge. When he entered the bridge, all the members of his team were already there. After completing some essential tasks and mechanical checkups, he flew the ship safely to the sky. It smoothly cut

through the thin air of Mars into the space and sped with a
high velocity toward the specified coordinates – at least 200
million kilometers away.

# Chapter 14

Sitting inside the bridge it was next to impossible to guess how fast the spaceship moved through the dark space. Pete was trying to figure out the direction from the coordinates. He had never gone that far before. Jupiter was about 3.7 AU (astronomical unit) from Mars – about 500 million kilometers (300 million miles). Between these two planets was an asteroid belt filled with thousands of thousand rocks of various sizes and some dwarf planets. Though the possibility of getting hit by any of them was very remote, but still it presented them with an additional problem. Why did Wolf head in that direction and not anywhere else? Pete wondered. If they moved at the highest speed it would take twenty- two hours to reach at the coordinates that Wolf had provided. That was more than enough time to come up with some kind of plan to tackle Wolf.

Rico stayed close to him. He was exceptionally intelligent for a robot and could figure out what Pete was thinking without even asking him. Little later, Jason and Michelle also joined them. They started to work on to find a way to outsmart Wolf.

Instead of asking the young group to join them, Pete encouraged them to group up and come up with an alternative plan. He had a simple goal in mind. He wanted to keep them busy. It worked. Not only they got busy, they also got pretty noisy. They occupied several tables at the back of the bridge and took turns to explain their respective plans. The only problem was nobody liked nobody else's plan. Every few minutes they burst into arguments. Soon they even divided into factions. Jing Jing and Mila packed up against Larisa and Taz. Overall, a very chaotic situation.

Michelle didn't like so much noise. She was clearly annoyed. Pete smiled. "Let them do it. They are young. They need to express themselves."

Michelle raised her eyebrow. "I have never seen such a soft hearted captain like you," she said.

Pete chuckled. "We are not the army. The more freedom we have, the more effective we'll be. Don't forget we are detectives. Yes, sometimes we have to tackle dangerous situations, but our primary goal is to solve mysteries. That is why I try not to impose anything on my crews. It had always worked. Think about you and Jason."

"We had never been that noisy, wouldn't you say? I just think there should be some regulations around etiquette."

"They are a well behaved noisy bunch. What's so wrong with that?" Pete smiled.

"You are the Captain. Do whatever you think best."

Pete chuckled. He enjoyed these little arguments with Michelle. "I guess you are not enjoying working with me."

"Don't be ridiculous!"

Michelle took her eyes of Pete and fixed them on the computer. Pete glanced at Jason. Any young man could easily figure out that Michelle had deep feelings for Pete. Pete often feared that Jason may be hurting inside. He didn't show anything right now. Rico was examining the computer generated plan with utmost attentiveness. Jason looked at the screen with equal seriousness. Pete quietly let go a breath of sigh and joined them in the analysis. Sometimes he wondered if he had met Michelle before Jason, would things be different. Who could say?

The main reason for Taz to get into arguments with Mila was that her every plan started and ended with shootings and killings. He, on the other hand, wanted to plan things in a way so that least amount of harm was done to life and property while still being effective. Obviously, Mila cared very little for such *nonsense* – that's how she put it. Not only she was scolding him every few seconds, but also took every opportunity to remind him that he knew nothing about battles and she could alone beat the daylight out of a dozen boys like him. Things were bound to go downward after such threatening remarks. Taz objected and Mila had become even more aggressive. Larisa came in his rescue. Not surprisingly, they hadn't been able to come up with anything solid even after two hours of constant bickering. There were two different things to consider – to rescue the two hostages, and to get Pete out of Wolf's ship safely after the exchange. Instead of pondering about such things Mila was all ready to attack wolf's ship with blazing cannons.

Dan called about three hours after they had started. Pete expected his call much earlier. Dan sounded slightly nervous.

"I spoke to Gary," He said gravely. "Is Mila with you?"

"Yes. Gary kind of insisted," Pete kept his voice down. He didn't want Mila to hear this.

"Gary is already a shipwreck. Take care of her. She is not anything like her dad."

"Rico is here as well," Michelle quickly said. While Mila was away from them, Rico was sitting next to the phone.

"I don't work as a spy," Rico quickly said.

"Gary knows very well how I feel about him," Dan said without being dithered. "Did Wolf contact you?"

"Nope. I don't think he is going to contact too soon," Pete said.

"What is the plan?"

"We are working on it. It's difficult to make a plan

without having any specific information. I am assuming he would try to exchange the hostages using a capsule. But there's no way to know what's going on in his mind. We'll have to play the waiting game."

"What are you planning to do once you become his prisoner? That's the one I need to know in details. I don't want that moron disappear taking you with him. Where would I look for you in this vast space?"

"No idea. I am kind of hoping he isn't going to hurt me right away. If I get a little time, I'll be able to find a way out."

"You are hoping?" Dan sounded almost cynical.

"I am confident I'll be able to figure something out," Pete said without much confidence in his voice. He didn't want Dan to panic.

"Do you need anything?" Dan didn't believe him.

"No, not really. Let me know as soon as you find out anything else about Wolf."

"I'll. Your mother contacted me a little while ago. She'll probably call you on your private line soon."

"Really!" Pete was a little surprised. Did his mother remember anything? Otherwise why would she look for him? "Did she say anything?"

"No. Do you remember anything about your father?"

"Nothing. Saw his pictures. Mom didn't say much

about him, I didn't ask. Did you know him?"

"No. But I heard his name. Since I learned Wolf is looking for you, I checked on both of your parents. Your mother is a politician, everybody knows her. But I couldn't find much about your dad."

"I heard he was a government employee. Do you know which department he worked for?"

"Don't know. I have not seen anything anywhere. It appears that someone have wiped off all his records carefully. I asked your mother but she knows even less than what I know. I would suggest - call her up. To you, time and information is most valuable now. I am in the office. I can't go home until this matter is resolved. I wanted to send another ship to help you out but no budget. Money is tight. But in extreme situation, Gary shall help. The moron is asking for too much though. And that is with his daughter flying with you!"

"May be his hands are tied," Pete lowered his voice. He didn't want Mila to hear this.

"Maybe. This is what happens when you build an empire using other people's money," Dan said sarcastically before disconnecting.

A little later, Pete's personal phone rang. Pete walked out of the bridge to the hallway. "Mom!"

"Are you okay, son?"

"Yes mom. We are moving toward the coordinates that Wolf provided us. It'll take us at least another twenty hours."

"Pete, I wanted to tell you something about your father. His body was not buried or cremated after his death."

Pete was confused. "What do you mean?"

"Your father's body and brain had been preserved. I don't know where they kept him. Nobody told me anything about this. We were already divorced when he died, so I really didn't have any right to know. I am telling you what I heard from a very confidential source. I haven't said Dan anything about this. I don't know how much you trust him. You'll have to decide who you want to share this information with."

A series of thoughts passed through Pete's mind. The technology to preserve human body and brain had been around for many years, but there were rare cases where it actually was applied, at least in last fifty years or so. When a lot of rich people started to show interest in this technology, the governments of all the countries in the world got together and decided to take it out of the reach of general population. Since then, very few people were allowed to use this technology, primarily secured for scientific experiments. Brilliant scientists, writers, politicians were not frozen. A decision was taken collectively that human civilization should be allowed to proceed in a natural way.  Men should not try to change it. When one brilliant mind die another would definitely be born to replace it. That's how the world has always worked.

Now the question was why in the whole world an ordinary government engineer would be frozen? The main reason for freezing people was to keep a way open to enter into their brains, if needed. What was so important stored in the brain of Robert Brown that he had to be frozen?

"Pete? Are you on the line?" Sicily asked.

"Yes mom. I am here. Thinking. Was it a government decision?"

"I have no idea. The only thing I can say is that unless a very high level politician wanted this wouldn't have happened. I think you should seek BSD's help.  You still have enough time in hand. If Dan wants, he can definitely help you. Do you trust him?"

"Is there any reason not to?"

"No particular reason. Just a precaution. There are all kinds of groups on Earth. No way to know who is working for whom. That's why we have to be very careful. As a politician, I have to be even more careful. I don't know Dan that well. You do. You would know what type of person he is."

"I trust him with my life mom."

"In that case, do not waste any time. You know what you must do."

"I know. You be careful. If you have any problem, let Dan know."

"I'll be fine. Don't worry about me. Take care, son."

Sicily disconnected abruptly. It was clear that she was worried. Pete was truly surprised. Why was she saying this to him after all these years? No doubt she wanted Pete to somehow get to his father's frozen body and find out any important information may be hidden with him. Was it possible that she knew something that nobody else did? Dan did not find anything after surfing through the world's information banks. It only meant one thing – somebody or some group wiped off all the information about his father, exactly what Dan was suspecting. Who could they be? Did his mom know more than what she revealed? Very unlikely.

Now the question was how to go near Robert's frozen body? The only person he could ask for help without compromising his safety was Dan. But could he trust Dan completely? Pete thought about it for a bit. The way Dan had nurtured him for the last six years if he (Pete) couldn't trust him (Dan), there was none he could.

Dan listened quietly. Once Pete stopped he thoughtfully said," I had some kind of suspicion for long time now. I remember hearing something about it a while ago. Didn't find anybody who could confirm this. If your mom is giving you this information then it can't be false. But there are a couple of problems. First, why was he frozen? Second, where is he kept? It won't be easy to find out. May also be dangerous. Not everybody get to be frozen. You already know that. I am surprised that your mom doesn't know more."

"I trust mom. I am sure she told me everything she knows," Pete said.

"Okay, let me check it out. We don't have too much time. At most twenty hours. I wish I had this information earlier. Anyway, you'll hear from me soon."

Dan disconnected. He needed to dig deep and had no time to waste. Both of them knew how much careful he needed to be. If there was a powerful group involved in Pete's father's death then the moment they would know that Dan was poking his nose into this, they would get cautious. Dan could even put himself at risk. Good thing was Dan had many trusted friends spread around the world who he could rely on.

Rico, Michelle and Jason were kneeling over a computer generated plan and were busy doing some analysis. As Pete entered the bridge all three of them looked at him. Pete had been away for a while and clearly they were dying to know the latest developments. If Rico wasn't present, Pete would have openly discussed the matter. He trusted Michelle and Jason. Rico was a Smartman who worked for Gary. He couldn't be trusted. Pete had reservations about Gary. He was a capable man with some serious motivation. Many had doubt and suspicion about his activities. He could have programmed Rico to meet his own needs. Dan did not trust him at all. Pete hadn't experienced anything bad yet, but there was no telling what Gary had in his mind.

"Is everything okay?" Michelle asked.

"I had some new info. I passed them on to Dan. Let's see if he can help us out," Pete said without revealing the secret.

"If he can't who can?" Jason said.

Pete nodded. "True. How is our escape plan going?"

Rico shook his head lightly. Which meant it wasn't going anywhere. He looked thoughtful and didn't say anything. Pete examined the plan. It had progressed a lot from where he had left. Because they had no way to know several important factors, the plan became very complex. They had to keep in mind all the possibilities. It wasn't easy to predict what Wolf was going to do. Rico knew some stuff about Wolf but that wasn't enough. What kind of distance would Wolf want to maintain during the exchange? What did he consider a safe distance? If capsules were used then there needed to be at least a minute or two of distance between the two spaceships. Would Wolf go for one minute or two minutes or something in between? In the space a capsule could be flown 160 kilometers (100 miles) per second. A distance of one minute translated to roughly 10,000 kilometers. Two minutes would double that up to 20,000 kilometers. They roughly assumed that the distance would be in between 10 to 20 thousand kilometers – that was a large range.

The primary goal was to snatch Pete away from Wolf after the hostage exchange was complete. To try anything tricky during the exchange would put the hostages under too much risk. Wolf would come ready. He would definitely have a solid strategy to make sure that Pete had little room to wiggle.

After a brief discussion one thing they decided unanimously that the exchange would be allowed to go through uninterruptedly. Once Wolf had Pete in his ship, he would probably try a quick escape. There was no way to know where he might be heading to, but it wasn't going to be Mars that much can be assumed safely. Could they chase him down with Space Tiger? Logically yes, but there was a big but. They would have to know where Wolf was heading to. Without prior knowledge, it would become very difficult if not totally impossible, to track him down in this vast space. Wolf might have top of the line scramblers to avoid detection by radar. Pete could take a tiny transmitter with him but Wolf would definitely do a thorough scan and find it.

The young group that gathered at the rear of the bridge was diligently working on their plan. Pete noticed things were still pretty chaotic there which clearly meant they hadn't been able to come to an agreement yet. Not unusual for kids of that age. It would take them some time to learn the most important thing about teamwork – to focus on the cause and not on ego. A grin popped up between his lips momentarily. He had been doing this since he was only sixteen. These kids were even younger! Someday they would do all the impossible things.

Taz and company could not go too far because they were unable to convince Mila to veer at all from her original plan. She continued to insist on her plenty of battle experiences and their lack of it. In a way she was right. She was not only quite experienced in battle techniques but was also pretty good at it. Nevertheless, that was no reason for her to undermine her companions. Instead of trying to work with them, she kept on pushing ahead with her opinion. This obviously didn't go very well with the rest who kept on pointing out gaping holes in her plan, which she did not admit.

Taz tried to be calm wondering how to break the

deadlock. Mila wasn't paying any attention to him or anybody else, but especially him. Every time he opened his mouth she barked at him and made no reservation in reminding him that he was no better than a milk fed baby and it would be better if he didn't open his mouth. Taz didn't mind much. Word didn't bite. However, Larisa wasn't as accommodating when Mila called her a novice. Larisa was not only older than her she actually had some experience in battle fields. She responded bitterly and they fought about it for a little bit with their voices lowered. Jing Jing had no clue how to handle such situation. He looked helpless and shrugged at regular intervals as if that was going to solve this problem.

# Chapter 15

Dan called exactly an hour later. Pete stepped out to the hallway again. This time he took further precaution and walked all the way back of the spaceship. He shouldn't be forgetting that Rico was a Smartman. He didn't really know what kind of power Rico had, but if he was able to increase his hearing power that wouldn't be surprising.

Dan brought up the subject himself. "Where is Rico?"

Pete was a little surprised. He wasn't sure why Dan suddenly brought up Rico. "Rico is in the bridge. I am outside in the corridor. All the way end. Why?"

"Good to be careful. He might have special hearing power."

"I was just wondering about that too. Even if he has, he couldn't possibly hear anything from where I am. I don't know if he can intercept the messages, but I doubt if he would be able to decipher them."

"True. The type of brain power needed to decipher these messages no Smartman have it, no matter how advance they are. Anyway, don't want to sound too suspicious but I really didn't expect Gary to send Mila and Rico with you."

"He is really disturbed about Wolf," Pete said. "He

doesn't want him to cause any more trouble in Mars."

"In plain words, he has sent Rico to kill Wolf. If it can be done at your presence, there will be no legal issues. Not sure why he sent his daughter."

"Have you met his daughter?"

"I did, couple of years ago, when she was on Earth. A total brat. Gary can't control her. Anyway, let's talk business. I got some information. Didn't speak to your mother. I doubt if she would tell me anything new. Anyway, I found where your father is. He was frozen, alright. I couldn't find out who requested it. There got to be a record somewhere, I just don't know where to look."

"Where have they kept him?" Pete asked.

"Library of Medical Science, New York City, with most of the other frozen subjects," Dan said.

Pete had never been there but knew enough to realize the challenge. It was one hundred and thirty storied building located in Manhattan. General public had access but only to a few zones out of the total ten. A handful of people were authorized to visit all the zones. Even the directors were not part of that elite group. American government had appointed a group of five people as auditors. Only they had the authority to visit any zone."

"I think your father has been kept in a high security zone," Dan said. "But I do not know exactly which one. I am kind of afraid to ask too many questions. There are many criminals on Earth who are always plotting to steal information from there. Billions of dollars worth of businesses are at stake. That is why, anybody – high rank officials, politicians, even the presidents are investigated if they start to show too much interest."

"How can we get to him?" Pete asked, almost knowing Dan wouldn't have called if he didn't already have some kind of plan.

"There is a way. But before we discuss that we must decide exactly what we want."

"Agreed," Pete said. When his mother gave him the information, all he wanted was to verify it. Now that it was confirmed, he needed to think about the next step. He sort of knew what he had to do, but still it was important to have a clear plan before moving ahead.

"I got to know why Wolf is looking for me. Did he have any kind of rivalry with dad? Dad was in Mars. Wolf was there too. There may be something in dad's memory. The question is how to connect with his brain? To my knowledge, the frozen brains are kept in a sleeping state and are accessible."

"That's what I heard too," Dan said. "I have a friend – a neuroscientist. He explained this once to me drawing tons of images. It is definitely possible to connect to your father's brain."

"Great!" Pete said. "If we can somehow access his brain and find any information about Wolf that's perfect; if not, there'll be one less thing to worry about."

"To tell you the truth," Dan gravely said, "I have a feeling you'll find a lot of highly confidential information."

"I suspect that too," Pete admitted. "Otherwise, why would he be frozen? Mom must have guessed something as well. Now the question is how to connect?"

"Have you heard about the Dummy Project?" Dan asked.

"A little," Pete said. "Something to do with remotely controlling a robot."

"Not a real robot. More like a robot body with little brain. They can be controlled using cell phones. I am going to send you the software. It'll allow you to control the movement and speech of the dummies."

"Can't we do it in any other way?" Pete hesitantly said. He didn't want to risk messing things up trying to use a sophisticated technology for the first time.

"There are many ways but none of them are safe," Dan said. "I can hire somebody on Earth. There are many organizations who rent out ex-army or ex-marines for jobs like this. But before I can hire anybody, I must check his background. We don't have time for that. You know government spies are always watching me. If I get caught, I can end up in jail. On the other hand, dummies are pretty safe. Even if you get caught, nobody would know your identity. Those robots have no memory. They'll have no information about you."

"Understood, but how are you going to get the dummies without leaving a trail behind?" Pete asked.

"I think in advance. I had bought some of these robots using a special channel, with false identity. I have been doing some experiments on them."

"Genius!" Pete could not hide his excitement. "However, how am I going to reach him through the heavy security?"

Dan laughed. "Even a needle has an opening. I know somebody who can help you to get in. Don't ask me anything else."

"When should we start?" Pete could hardly wait.

"Whenever you are ready. But you won't be able to do this alone. Take company. I am sending you the software right now. Install it into your intelligent headphones. It'll synchronize with your brain. Test it. I'll call after an hour. Be ready."

"Can we get caught?" Pete asked.

"No," Dan said. "When at risk just disconnect. The robots will be left behind. They have no identity, as I said."

Before hanging up Dan gave a bad news. "I tried to contact your mother. I couldn't find her. Nobody knows where she is. I thought you should know this."

Pete was shocked. He never thought his mother could be at risk. "Do you think she is okay?"

"I have no reason to think otherwise but you never know," Dan chose his words carefully. He disconnected.

Pete checked the address once more. He didn't know New York City that well. He was from Michigan. The primary reason he visited New York was to board the spaceships. He drove for sometime before pulling into a narrow road in Astoria flanked with small old houses on both sides with reasonably good cars on the driveways. That meant, the residents weren't exactly affluent but they weren't poor by any standard. He thought the road was too narrow for safe driving, especially with cars parked along one side of the road. Every time another car came from opposite direction he had to stop and allow it to pass by.

He was connected to a Dummy Joe. The male zombie robots were briefly called Dummy Joe, while the females were called Dummy Jane. The robot he was given was big, not less than six and half feet tall. The black population was predominant here; hence Dan picked a black dummy for him. That way he won't be identified easily. Rico was sitting beside him. He was also riding a black dummy. Both of them were well dressed in trousers, shirts and ties. Cops had frequent movement in the area. The last thing they wanted was to get their (cop's) attention.

It wasn't hard to find the place. After going about a mile they found the bungalow style small house on their right. It was just as old as all the other houses with weeds running over the front yard. Clearly nobody had taken care of it for a long time. There were no lights inside the house. Didn't look like anybody lived there. But how was that possible? Pete wondered. Dan would have never sent him to a place without solid information.

He drove past the house for about fifty feet and parked the car on the curb beside a large tree. There were street lights at regular intervals on the sidewalk. The lights weren't very bright but eyes worked. Pete remembered seeing a few police cars patrolling the neighborhood. He sat quietly inside the car for a little bit and checked around him carefully. When he thought it was safe, he climbed out of the car. Rico looked at him questioningly. Should he come along? Pete thought for a moment and asked him to stay inside the car. If Pete did not return in twenty minutes, he should go look for him.

The big trees that lined both sides of the road stood like tall umbrellas. Pete tried to stay in their shadows as he walked toward the house. It was a late summer night, the neighborhood was pretty quiet. Everybody must have gone to bed. There were some cars and isolated pedestrians on the main roads, but nothing was moving on this street. Pete was happy. While he wasn't exactly a small man, he was having real difficulties adjusting himself in this big body. Dan had warned him that in the beginning it was going to be very uncomfortable. However, the software was very good. It transmitted his brain waves quite smoothly to the dummy. To make it walk, all Pete had to do was to think that he was walking. Same technique worked for all other movements.

However, there was an added complexity here due to the physical distance of Pete and Rico from Earth. They were about 160 million kilometers away. It took radio signal to travel that distance about eight - nine minutes, which meant direct controlling was out of question. During software installation some logical patterns of their brains were transferred to Earth to a secret server. Even though there were no plans to have other members to join the operation, Dan instructed them to complete this step. This could save plenty of time later, if for whatever reason, they had to participate.

Pete walked through an iron gate and stepped into the small front yard of the house. Looking back, he saw Rico sitting quietly inside the car watching Pete on the side mirror.

Pete thought hard before deciding to bring Rico with him. A Smartman could be much more dependable than a human at time of need. In addition, any damage suffered by a Smartman was considered less significant than a human injury. Rico knew it and didn't seem to mind. Whether Gary had sent him for any particular reason or not Pete didn't know. He hadn't seen any indication of anything fishy yet. It was useless to ask Rico. Not only Smartmans could lie, they were very good at it.

He found a calling bell beside the door. It was white at some point of time in the past. As he pressed it a bell rang inside several times. Moments later a light was turned on in the living room. Somebody walked to the door and opened it. He was a Chinese man of small stature, unshaven, uncombed hair, in his sleeping dress. He silently signaled Pete to get inside the house. Pete walked in. The man closed the door silently behind him.

"You are late," The man spoke in clear English.

"You are Larry Ming?" Pete asked.

"Yes. You are Pete. I spoke to Dan just about a minute ago. I thought you might have gotten lost. Sit."

Larry did not try to shake hands. It was a tiny living room with a small sofa accompanied by a round table and couple of wooden chairs. Everything was tasteful, clean. The outside of the house did not reflect anything about the inside. Pete sat on a chair. Larry took out a device that looked like a phone and sat beside him. He looked at Pete with keen eyes. "These dummies are not too bad. They look just like humans."

He pressed some keys on the device and projected a picture on the wall. "This is the Library of Medical Science. Have you ever been there?"

"No."

"In that case pay attention to the next slides. Where is your companion?"

"In the car."

He projected another picture on the wall. "First floor. Everybody must enter the building through here, even the employees. There are several emergency exits; all of them are heavily guarded. Nobody can come in or go out without proper identification. The powerful electronic security system is complemented by additional robot and trained human security guards."

"Do you know which zone they kept my dad in?" Pete asked.

"I do." Larry projected another image.

Dan had already given Pete some information about this man. He was a senior Security Guard Controller of the Library of Medical Science building. There were several of them and their job was to control the robot guards. Many institutions were following the same path lately. They bought robot guards and hired trained human controllers. The security controllers had to go through very detailed background checks. How Dan found this man was a mystery. Pete had asked but Dan sort of avoided answering and wanted him not to get too concerned about it. Pete understood Dan did not want to reveal the identity of his close allies or friends. Today he trusted Pete, but who knew what would happen tomorrow?

Larry projected another image on the wall. A corridor; wide, carpeted, lined up doors on both sides gave an impression that there were many rooms. The end of the corridor could not be viewed clearly. The floor number was not written anywhere. None of the doors had any number on them either. "All the Frozens are kept here. Several in each room. Not all rooms have same type or level of security. They are classified based on importance. As a result, some of them have low security while some others are so highly secured that even president of America won't be able to enter without prior approval."

"Approval from whom?"

"Board of auditors. Difficult to get. Very few outsiders have been permitted until now."

"Why so much security?" Pete asked. He sort of guessed the answer but wanted to find out if Larry would give any new information.

Larry looked at him, a little annoyed. "Why are you assuming that your father is the only mysterious frozen person there?"

Pete shrugged. He had no interest in investigating the Frozens right now. He would be very happy to be able to reach just his father. He did not respond to Larry's question. He had no desire to piss Larry off.

"Can you guess which floor is this?" Larry asked.

"I don't see any signs anywhere. But I am guessing it won't be too high from ground. Possibly fourth or fifth floor."

"Wrong. It is underground, forty feet below. There is a main tunnel and a backup tunnel to ensure that the Frozens can be moved easily, if such a situation arises. Very few people know this. We'll have to enter the building using one of those two tunnels. If we go near the main gate, hundreds of images will be taken and stored in the system with all kind of security checks happening instantly."

"We don't have much time in hand. Will we be able to do this relatively quickly?" Pete asked, little unsure.

"I have already arranged for it, but there are still some problem points. Only two of you won't be able to handle everything. We'll need some additional help."

"What do you mean by problem points?" Pete asked.

Larry showed another image of an underground train station. "Science building subway station. The door to the main tunnel is from here. Only guards with special security cards are allowed through that door. I've full access. No worries there. To enter the main building, we must go through an electronically secured steel door, located at the end of the tunnel. I'll be able to help you with that. The problem is, once we step inside the tunnel we have only half an hour to finish. If my card is detected checked in longer than half an hour, a signal will be sent to the security. They would try to contact me immediately. If they find anything suspicious, they would override all my access. What that means is, we'll be stuck inside and eventually captured."

"Is half an hour enough time for us?" Pete asked.

"Yes, if everything goes smoothly. But there is no way to predict that. I have access to almost everywhere, but there can still be trouble. That's why we need to have a backup plan ahead of time.  We need your team mates. Here's what I am thinking…"

In the next ten minutes two of them scrutinized Larry's plan. They made some changes. It was decided that Pete and his team would meet Larry at the subway station in an hour.

Pete quickly stepped out of the house, walked back to the car and got in. He gave Rico the address of the subway station and signaled him to drive. Rico pulled away silently. He was curious but he did not ask any questions. He knew Pete would explain everything when the time was right. Pete called up Dan instantly and described their plan. He needed to confirm that they were not stepping into a trap.

# Chapter 16

When Pete, Rico, and Jason walked into the Science building subway station, it was 1 in the morning. The sprawling station was brightly lit with a considerably large crowd inside. Many companies had night shifts. As a result, traffic at night had increased steadily. The frequency of the trains was slightly lower than daytime but still arrived and departed every five to ten minutes. A big bright billboard showed the arrival and departure times, updating every few seconds.

Pete walked all the way down the platform along with Rico and Jason, who was riding a young, strong looking Caucasian male's dummy. Jason would team up with Rico and stay out as guards. If for any reason Larry and Pete couldn't get out of the science building within half an hour, building security would try to contact Larry. If a response is not received immediately or anything looked suspicious, they would raise an internal alarm and send cops to the tunnel. Rico and Jason would have to try their best to delay the cops without causing any serious injuries or loss of life.

As they climbed down the stairs, they could see Larry standing inside a convenience store. He had a magazine in his hand, which he pretended to read. Pete walked inside the store and stood close to him. Rico and Jason stayed outside on the platform. Larry couldn't be sure, but he believed there was an intelligent electronic monitoring system installed in the station to keep an eye on everybody who came in and out of the station and to send an internal alarm to the building security office if it detected anything suspicious. To his knowledge, there were no human or robot guards here. He had never seen any.

"What now?" Pete muttered.

"Ask your team to create the diversion," Larry almost whispered. "Once they get going, I'll wait thirty seconds and then start walking. Follow me. Thirty feet past the washrooms you'll see a locked door. I'll open it and walk in. Follow me."

"Okay," Pete said.

"Stay calm," Larry mumbled and moved away.

Pete bought a newspaper and slowly walked out of the store. He looked around, trying to be as normal as possible. There were no cops or security guards anywhere. Pete called Dan and asked him to send in the diversion team. Dan was working as the controller for this mission and had set up a highly secure phone number for all communication.

Michelle, Jing Jing and Larisa were waiting in a café in Manhattan. It was very early in the morning but the café was mostly filled. Three of them had occupied a table at one corner and were waiting eagerly for the signal from Dan.

When Dan finally called, a little after 1 AM, and asked them to make the move, they wasted no time and rushed out of the café to the street. Michelle and Larisa were riding dummies of young Hispanic women. Jing Jing was riding a dummy Joe of a black man and was carrying a small but very powerful boom box. Even at that hour there was significant foot traffic on the sidewalks. Some were walking home after returning from work in subways or busses; others were heading to work in the late night shifts. Like most large cities of the world, life in New York City never stopped.

Three of them continued to walk toward the Library of Medical Science building, as fast as they could. It was not as much fun to walk or run with a dummy. They were all struggling. None of them had any experience with this technology and could barely walk in the beginning. After some diligent practice things got kind of easier. But still, it was nothing near being comfortable. Jing Jing seemed to have the worst time.

"Are you okay?" Larisa inquired. "You are hobbling."

"I know," Jing Jing bitterly said. "I feel weird. Can't feel my legs."

"Neither can I," Michelle said. "Just make sure you don't fall. You are the star of the show."

"You think you'll be able to do the moves?" Larisa

said, doubtfully.

"I don't know. I'll have to try my best. Dummies are no fun," Jing Jing muttered.

"Don't think about the legs," Michelle said. "It's all in your mind. I know you can do it.  We can't back off now. We are almost there."

Minutes later, they walked past the enormous gate of the Library of Medical Science building and walked inside the lobby through the revolving door with as much confidence as they could master.

General people had around the clock access to many parts of this building. Beside the main lobby they could visit designated areas on various floors. All visitors had to register at the front desk. In one corner of the lobby was an easily detectable section built with special glass that allowed only one way vision. Insiders could see through but the outsiders saw nothing. This was the main security office of the building. Anybody who entered the building through the main gate got there images taken by several hidden cameras spread throughout the lobby. The images were then checked against several databases of people to find their identity and criminal records. If there was any hit or if anybody looked suspicious, the security guards would take immediate action.

Dan had confirmed that the dummies they were riding had no resemblance to anybody with criminal records.

He checked. But then, these matters were impossible to control. There was no way to tell if the security system would identify one or more of the dummies as suspicious and raise alarms. In case something like that happened, or anything else that could be considered dangerous, they were instructed to disconnect from their dummies immediately. Dan didn't think security would be able to find any information even if they had the dummies.

The lady sitting at the reception had just opened her mouth to greet them, when they decided to start the madness. At this hour most of the public programs were closed but many scientists and their associates were working in various departments. Several dozens of people could be seen hanging inside the lobby, mostly on break. A hundred feet behind the reception was another gate, much smaller. This allowed entry to the actual floors and was guarded by several heavily armed guards.

"Start?" Larisa asked.

"Start," Michelle said.

They both looked at Jing Jing who placed the boom box on the counter and pressed a small button starting a shockwave of musical storm. The deafening sound had the elderly clerk jump and run away from them. Michelle, Larisa, and Jing Jing had come prepared. They quickly took out ear plugs, wore them and then started to dance. Within moments it became clear that Larisa and Michelle weren't much of a dancer but Jing Jing was another story. Just looking at the way he moved his arms and legs and shook his body it was quite evident that he was an expert in street dancing. He somersaulted in the air, spun on the ground on one hand, did routines on his toes like ballet dancers mesmerizing the small audience, who were present in the lobby. Not even ten seconds had passed, when the door of the security section opened and came out rushing several security guards. The dancing trio quickly scattered around the large lobby to avoid a quick capture. One guard went to look for the boom box while the rest chased the three.

Michelle was worried that at time of need their dummies would not cooperate, but in reality it worked out much better. She was relieved. They had an important role to play. Failure wouldn't be an option.  As the guards chased them around the lobby, they ran and dodged much faster than she thought was possible. The dummies were flexible, tough and strong, exactly what they needed to keep the security guards running at their tails.

Larisa was handling her dummy very well. Watching her sliding past between the legs of a guard, Michelle could barely stop herself from breaking into laughter. Jing Jing was definitely having most of the fun at the expense of the poor guards, who collided, fell, slipped as they tried to grab him.

He rolled front and back at his will, slid, jumped, and did all kind of fascinating stuff to avoid getting captured by them.

When things started to look getting slightly out of hand, more guards poured out to help their colleagues. A few of them were carrying guns – both laser and regular, though none showed any interest in using them, at least not just yet. After several lawsuits filed against public injuries and deaths in the hands of police and security guards, rules had been changed to make sure almost all shootings were done using special low-impact bullets and low powered lasers. None being life threatening, government expected the number of law suits to go down drastically. Michelle and her team were aware of this and they were taking full advantage of the situation. They were not armed, so there was very little chance that the guards would consider using gun power against them.

As the commotion continued, Police were informed. Michelle could hear the wailing sound of the police cars approaching fast. That was good. Michelle checked her watch as she took an abrupt turn causing a female guard to stumble ahead. Almost ten minutes had passed since they entered the lobby. Another few minutes and they could call it a night.

Larry passed his ID card over a card reader located

next to a heavy steel door. Next, he had to put his hand on a flat screen and look into a small opening. The security system matched his ID with his hand prints and iris recognition system. It went smoothly as expected and the door opened up almost instantly. As a controller guard Larry had the authority to bring in maintenance workers in the facility. Pete, wearing a blue dress of a renowned and registered technical farm, followed him closely through the door. It closed behind them silently. As they stepped inside a long corridor they were greeted by a series of cameras placed strategically on the roof. Pete froze as several of the cameras moved and focused on his face.

Larry slapped him on the back assuring. "Nothing to worry," He whispered. "Your dummy is clean."

Pete slowly let go a big sigh. His heart had missed a beat. He tried to relax. Larry looked at ease, quite sure about his actions. They were standing at one end of an empty corridor that was several hundred yards long. Pete felt a touch of fear. What would happen if somebody came to the corridor right now? He would see both of them clearly. There was no place to hide.

"Which way?" Pete asked.

"Straight. There are no numbers on the doors. But they have electronic IDs. My scanner would show the room numbers. When the right room comes up I'll signal."

Pete walked ahead in long strides with Larry following him closely holding the scanner in his palm. As they went past dozens of closed doors Pete started to panic. They had very little time to get this done. He looked at Larry, who looked undeterred. He checked his scanner and shrugged calmly. Pete read it as a silent suggestion to keep moving. He knew they had already spent about ten minutes out of the 30 minutes limit. Several minutes had gone in the tunnel, which was much longer than what Pete had expected. He increased his pace.

After going past several more doors, finally Larry stopped before one. "This is the one. Wait. I'll open it." He held his security clearance card in front of a small electronic device attached to the door. It quietly slid aside. Once they entered the room, the door silently closed behind them. Pete wasn't sure exactly what he expected to see, but he couldn't help feeling slightly disappointed. It was a medium sized rectangular room, about fifty by fifty feet. Along the walls were large almirah like objects placed 10-15 feet apart from each other. They were built with hard opaque objects with no names or information written on them whatsoever. Each had a large digital display at the center of the front panel. In total there were seven almirahs in the room, Pete counted. He assumed they would have to somehow communicate to one of these almirahs holding his father's frozen body.

"Are these…" Pete didn't finish his question.

"Yes. They are called Boxes," Larry replied as he walked toward a Box located at the far end of the room. "They do have a scientific name but nobody uses that. Your father is in this corner. There is no tag outside but my scanner can read the code implanted inside the box."

Pete walked to the Box. It looked exactly same as all the other Boxes. "Where is my father's body?"

"Inside it. These things are high tech freezers. The body is kept exactly the way it was when he was alive. But some electronic mechanism is used to connect to his brain, which is alive but not active. All his memories are supposed to be intact. At least that's what the scientists believe. Let's connect."

Larry quickly pressed some buttons on the keyboard. A message popped up on the screen.

*"Do you want to connect with Robert Brown?"*

Between the two options, 'Yes' and 'No', Larry pressed the 'Yes' button.

The monitor showed, *"Connecting..."*

Within few seconds it declared that they were now connected to Robert Brown's brain. Pete wasn't sure exactly what being connected meant. There was no doubt he wasn't going to be able to speak to his father. What then?

Larry took out a small object from his pocket.

Storage chip. These things had become so tiny nowadays that it was hard to believe. Larry pushed the chip in a slot located on the side of the monitor. "During the procedure of freezing, the scientists pulled out all the information from the brain, whatever they could, and stored them in a separate disk. We have just connected to that disk, not to the actual brain. Only the scientists have the capability to do so. Our plan is to copy whatever we can from the disk and later analyze the data. We have about five minutes before we must leave or risk getting caught."

He pressed some more buttons to start the copying.

Pete felt restless. Being inside a strange dummy, standing quietly in the middle of a room with seven mysterious looking boxes, and waiting for a copy job to complete which supposed to contain some of his father's memories – all of it felt quiet unreal. Who knew what Michelle and the two trainees were doing at the lobby upstairs. They had a risky job as well. If they got caught that could also be disastrous. "How long would it take to copy?" He asked Larry, who patiently waited.

"No idea. It depends on how much information there is. It can take couple of minutes to half an hour. A human brain can contain a lot of information."

A message showed up on the monitor, "Copying. Four minutes left."

There was only one thing to do – wait. Larry was totally calm, confident. Pete could not be so fearless. "Can I ask you something?" He said.

"Shoot," Larry said.

"Who do you work for?" Pete bluntly asked. "What you are doing is pretty dangerous stuff."

"I don't work for anybody," Larry quietly said. "I am part of a large group. Our goal is to protect the interest of ordinary citizens. Can't say any more. Dan is our friend. We help each other. Our members are spread out all over the world and beyond."

"Does that mean you had no connection with my father?"

"Right. I didn't even know your father."

"Then why are you helping me?"

"For Dan, of course! He is a good man. He always does the right thing. Not easy for somebody in his position. We can't say 'no' to a decent man."

"Do you know somebody named 'Wolf'?" Pete asked, deciding to give it a try. The monitor showed exactly one and half minutes left.

"Dan already asked me about him. Unfortunately we have no knowledge of him."

Another minute or so passed, which felt like eternity. The copying finally completed. Larry quickly took the chip out and handed it over to Pete. "Let's get out of here," he said.

He shut off the monitor and hurried toward the door. Pete remained glued to him. Larry's magic card allowed them to get out and step in the corridor. Larry pointed at the elevator nearby. "Go to upstairs. Your team members in lobby must have already spread out the smoke bombs. Blast them as planned and get out of here. I'll be behind you. If you get into trouble, I'll try my best to help you."

Pete did not waste any time. He ran toward the elevator. Sensing his presence an elevator quickly came down. Pete rushed in. Larry signaled that he was taking the next one. Pete set the elevator for the ground floor and connected with Michelle on the phone.

"Michelle! Michelle!" he whispered.

Michelle responded amid a lot of noise. "Everything is ready. Go ahead, blast them."

"Great! You guys can now disconnect from the dummies," Pete said.

"Not before you get out of the building," Michelle said. "If we get caught nothing would happen. We can escape leaving the dummies behind. But you need to physically get out of here to transport the chip."

Pete knew she was right. "What's all that noise about?"

"They are chasing us around, of course. Very chaotic here."

Michelle disconnected. The main goal for three of them was to spread out tiny sand like smoke bombs all over the lobby. Pete would be able to activate the smoke bombs using his phone. These bombs were specially made to blow up with loud noises and generate heavy dense smoke, though totally harmless. Their main advantage was that they were small and hard to detect.

Pete blew off the smoke bombs from inside the elevator. He could hear a series of loud blasts. Few moments later, when he carefully stepped out of the elevator on the ground floor, it was already covered with dense black smoke. The smoke bombs were still going off like an orchestrated effort, from different parts of the lobby, sometimes weakly sometimes vigorously – almost like fireworks. People were running around for safety. The emergency alarm went off shrieking at maximum strength. He could hardly see anything through the dense smoke and almost guessed his way toward the main gate. After about fifty yards he turned right. Many scientists who were working inside the labs located in different floors of the building had streamed out. He ran into a group that rushed out of an emergency staircase. Looking back he vaguely saw Larry following him, keeping a good distance. Larry shouted, asking him to run. Pete ran. The smoke wasn't going to last forever. He had at most two-three minutes before it started to thin out. He needed to get out of the building before that.

After going another hundred yards he could see the security gate that allowed access into the floors. Under normal circumstances several armed guards would be guarding it. Pete approached with caution. He could not see any guards at the gate, but his vision was very limited. He could barely see ten fifteen feet ahead.

"Keep going," he could hear Larry speaking almost to his ears. "Go through the security gate and walk straight to the main entrance and out," Larry said.

He then shouted something to the other guards. Pete could hear the pounding of his heart as he tried to stay calm, walking through the security gate. Nobody demanded him to stop as he stepped into the lobby – submerged in dense black smoke. He tried to remember the layout of the lobby from memory. People were running around like shadowy figures confusing his sense of direction. He could hear loud sirens approaching this way. Must be a dozen or more police cars. They needed to get out of there soon.

He dashed toward the area where he thought the main gate would be. He hit several objects including a few guards on his way, stumbled to the floor once but stood up quickly and continued to the main gate. As he closed on, he noticed to his dismay that one of the guards were trying to close the gate. Before he could decide what to do, Jing Jing came running and pushed the guard away. Michelle and Larisa were right next to him. Without wasting any more time they rushed out through the open gate into the sidewalk. The smoke had started to make its way outside, spreading quickly on the sidewalk and part of the street. The pedestrians had moved away from the place fearing harmful gases. They stood on the other side of the road and ogled to get a sense of what was going on inside the building.

The four of them ran a little further down the sidewalk to a waiting car and huddled into it. Rico was driving with Jason at the passenger seat. He pulled away fast and zoomed out of the area. Jason briefly described the events at the subway station. Police had arrived very quickly, as soon as the problem started. The two of them stayed in safe distance and used smoke bombs to hold the police up at least for ten minutes or so. After that they slipped out of the station, got into the car and came to pick them up.

Rico knew where to go. Dan had arranged for it ahead of time. He drove at a steady speed, not asking for any undue attention from law enforcers.

"What did you get?" Michelle asked once she caught her breath.

"My dad's memory," Pete showed the tiny chip.

"Hopefully this has the answer to all my questions."

# Chapter 17

Taz couldn't help but feel a certain level of pride to be the Pilot in Charge of Space Tiger. With the exception of Mila and him, all the rest had gone to the Earth on Dummies. Each of them wore a large set of intelligent headphones, which they were using to connect to the dummies remotely. Taz had no way to know exactly what was happening on Earth. Looking at the occasional facial expressions of excitement and fear in the faces of the team members who were riding dummies, he couldn't clearly figure out much. Mila probably wanted to go, because she had been very upset. Taz thought of cranking up a conversation with her but couldn't gather up enough courage.

"Why are you looking at me like that?" Mila snapped.

"Why are you so mad at me?" Taz protested.

"Don't be silly. I am not mad at you or anybody."

"That mission is dangerous. It's good that Pete didn't take you with them."

"What could possibly happen? Take off the headphone and you are safe. I really wanted to do this. It would have been my first time using a dummy."

"There will be other times," Taz tried to console her.

"Don't try to patronize me." Mila snapped.

"Sorry." That was the only safe thing Taz could think of saying.

Space Tiger was moving at a very high speed, though they felt nothing. It was like floating in a small boat in a dark and calm ocean. The entire sky glittered with stars. Jupiter was prominent with its moons. Sitting behind the switch panel Taz really enjoyed looking outside into the starry sky. May be this was why he loved to come to space. One could not imagine the depth and intensity of such views sitting on Earth. Mila had been sitting right next to him all this time, showed plenty of interest about all the buttons, panels and switches that could be used to control the spaceship. Taz knew how to fly a spaceship like this, most part of it, and was delighted to answer all her questions. However, he was careful enough not to allow her to actually touch anything on the control panel. He didn't want to take any risk.

"You are a little poetic," Mila said, breaking her short silence.

"Why do you say that?"

"You are watching the stars in a way as if this is the first time you are seeing them," Mila twisted her lips, almost smilingly.

"I like to watch stars, especially in a peach dark sky. Don't they look amazing?"

"Don't know. Maybe. Do you miss your family?"

"Yes, very much," Taz said, a little sadly. "You know, I was just thinking, maybe sometimes I am kind of mean to them. If anybody touches my stuff, I get very upset. I have two brothers. They are always causing trouble for me. I am the oldest, so I have to be patient. My parents really look up to me. They want me to be brilliant and extraordinary, you know, all the good things. I don't know if I can be that good. Anyway, I said too much. Sorry. Do you want to say anything about you?"

"My parents are divorced," Mila smiled bitterly. "I have no siblings. Mom lives on Earth. She really loves me but staying with her is so boring. Studies, sports, useless parties – after a month or so I start to go crazy. That's why I come here to live with dad. City of Mars is very exciting!"

"Where did you learn to fight like that?"

"In our game center! There is a virtual battle setup there. When I first came that's where I used to spend most of my time. At first dad didn't like it very much. But when he saw my skill, he was like – wow! He started to encourage me. Now I can fight better than many experienced fighters."

"There is no doubt about that. But I must say you are at the border line of being reckless. You need to slow it down a little bit before you get hurt or something."

"If I get hurt so be it. In a battle anybody can get

hurt."

"Aren't you afraid?"

"No. Why should I be afraid? When you are operating a ship are you afraid?"

"No. But those two are not the same."

"It's a question of being comfortable. Let's not talk about that anymore. How about we take Space Tiger out for a spin?"

"Spin? What do you mean by spin?" Taz was alarmed. He had very little trust in her. She was definitely capable of doing something very much unexpected.

"Spinning it, literally. Can we? Like an U.F.O.?"

"Possible," Taz cautiously said.

"Let's do it then."

"No, no, no. We shouldn't be doing anything like that. All of us can get into trouble." Taz was almost at his toes, ready to grab Mila in case she tried anything foolish. Mila broke into laughter.

"Why are you laughing? This is not funny," Taz weakly objected.

"Did you really think I was going to do something like that? Am I some kind of an idiot or something? You should have seen your face," Mila kept laughing.

Taz could not join her. He was rather feeling like a fool. But at the same time, deep inside, he was relieved. Mila was a girl with strong personality. If she persisted Taz would have difficulty stopping her. Apparently, she wasn't as reckless as she seemed to be.


Rico drove very carefully out of Manhattan. Pete had urged him several times to make sure that they didn't get any attention from the cops. As a result, he drove at the posted speed limit or less. When they finally arrived in the parking lot of an abandoned two storied house in Astoria, it was 2 am in the morning. Dan had arranged for this place ahead of time. The house was located inside an isolated alley. It was clear from the first sight that nobody had lived there for a while. About fifty feet away was a large structure of an abandoned mill of some kind with its walls spray painted with an assortment of gang names in large colorful letters.

The house looked beaten, dilapidated as if it would crumble down anytime. There was no sign of anybody living in the house but yet they took usual precautions and walked to the back door as quietly as they possibly could. With a little push of hand the rickety door opened up. Pete took out his flashlight and quickly checked inside. There were two sets of wooden stairs – one going up, other one to the half basement. Pete stepped inside and put his weight on the first step to the upstairs. It made a screeching noise, clearly giving an impression that it wouldn't be able to support their weights. He then checked the stairs to the basement, which looked much better. "They are not gonna collapse, are they?" Michelle whispered.

"No, these ones are strong," Pete said. He carefully climbed down to the basement. The old wood grumbled but withheld. Pete signaled others to come down, one at a time. It was an open basement with only one medium size window most of which was above ground. The glass panels were still intact; dirty but transparent enough to see through. If anybody approached the house from back alley they would be able to see the visitor. Pete tried the light switch. Nothing happened. No electricity. The line must have been disconnected long ago.

Michelle took out a battery operated camp light and pushed it on the wall where it stuck. Soft low intensity light. Even if anybody from the nearby neighborhoods looked this way, they probably wouldn't notice it. That was an important consideration. Pete didn't want anybody to get suspicious and get the police involved.

"What's next?" Jason asked.

Pete took out a quarter size chip from his pocket. "We need to analyze this."

"How?" Rico asked. "We need a special machine to read this chip."

"I thought Dan would arrange for that. Let me talk

to him," Pete said.

Before he could make the call, they saw a pair of headlights approaching the house. Apprehensive, Pete signaled everybody to move out of the window. The approaching car slowed down and parked next to their car. Moments later climbed out a small man. He looked around watchfully and slipped into the house through the backdoor.

"Pete! Pete!" he called in soft voice.

"Larry!" Pete responded. He went to the mouth of the stairs. "This way, Larry."

Larry carefully climbed down the stairs to the basement. "Are you guys alright?"

"Yes. We were a little worried. Haven't heard anything from you or Dan for a while."

"I had a little trouble when trying to get out of that building. The police had already arrived. Do you still have the chip? I brought the reader. Sometimes a lot of the information that is harvested from the brain is not very clear. Often it contains strange encryptions. Surprisingly enough, some studies suggest that the people with genetic connection, especially children, can somehow see through the encryption. Messages that took smart scientists months to decrypt, took them just hours. The perception is, genetically related people may share similar pattern of cognitive information storage and retrieval capabilities."

Larry stood next to Pete. "I know you don't have a whole lot of time but what we are going to do now must be done very carefully. It is a common observation that repeated access to the information somehow corrupts the data and makes them unreadable. So, we'll have to try to keep it as simple as possible."

Pete checked his watch. They still had enough time. They had spent about four hours to get the copy of his father's brain. They still had about sixteen hours before the exchange would take place. Now the question was would he find anything useful in the chip? He tried to remain optimistic. There was no other place he could look.

A few strange characters showed up on the screen. None of them belonged to any familiar alphabet.

"When machine do not know the mapping of something it spurts out some strange weird characters. Just press enter," Larry said.

Pete pressed enter on the virtual keyboard that kind of hung in the air. The strange characters immediately disappeared and bunch of neat small rectangle buttons lined up on the screen. Each of these buttons had English labels on them – politics, occupation, education etc. In total sixteen of them.

"Press on any of them. Let's find out what it shows," Larry said.

Pete picked the button 'Occupation' from the list. After a moment a stream of English letters quickly rolled through the screen from top to bottom. They could not read anything. This went on for five seconds before stopping abruptly. A page was displayed on the screen. It contained many texts with familiar words. In some areas there were big gaps. All the eyes were now fixed on the screen. But it was very difficult to find anything meaningful from so much content that looked like garbage. After browsing through several useless pages Pete finally saw something that made some sense. His father worked in a salt mine for some time. He had some memories about his experience there. One particular line attracted all of their attention:

*It's so dark! All the lights went off.*

*People are scared.   Not everybody*

*need to be afraid.*

A few lines of illegible characters later another series of words that made sense:

*Daylight again! Feels good. I really*

*want to see my son.*

A little later among some unrelated text another line:

*After that salt mine something*

*has happened to me. I don't want*

*to do this anymore.*

As a robot, Rico had better skill set than most

average humans in analyzing things like this. He had gone through the page in seconds. He detected the last part slightly after Pete had.

"Strange!" Rico muttered. "Have you seen it, Pete?"

Pete highlighted the line. "This one?"

"Yes. But why would he suddenly say such a thing? Let me check in my memory bank. I might find some additional information from the cloud data bank. Give me a few seconds. If I can find out how many accidents happened in salt mines in last few decades, I would probably be able to figure out which accident Robert is referring to."

Rico found the answer in moments. "In the year 2085 there was a big disaster in a salt mine in South Africa," he said. "Hundreds of workers were stuck in the mine for days. Total ten workers died. Some people believed those ten were members of a secret gang, who escaped from USA and hid in South Africa."

Pete looked at Larry questioningly. Larry shrugged. "I know nothing about this. May be your mother knows something."

"You know my mother?" Pete was surprised.

"Dan mentioned her," Larry briefly said. "Seems to me your father was working for a special department of the American government."

"Secret Service!" Larisa was all excited.

"Probably," Pete said. "I had no idea. May be that's why I never saw him around. The engineering consultancy thing was just a camouflage."

"We should continue to check the next pages. There may be other information hidden there," Larry rushed them. "You don't have enough time."

Pete agreed. There could be thousands of pages with useful information. Finding and analyzing them could be a very lengthy process. As they continued through the storage chip, his luck seemed to run out. The next hundreds of pages provided nothing meaningful.

"Do you know how the information is harvested from the brain?" Pete asked Larry.

"The scientists came up with some kind of procedures to collect and store information. Apparently that is not very advanced," Larry said, unhappily.

"Most of the stuff is garbage," Michelle said.

"We should check other categories," Rico said. "There's no way to know how the information got categorized during the harvesting process."

"Statistically it could take us years to go through all the data in that chip," Jing Jing said in a matter of fact way.

Pete agreed. Even if his father's memory contained any information on Wolf, it could take him long time to find it. But for now, that was the only viable option he had. He continued to browse through the pages. Every page contained at least a few thousand words. Unrelated, meaningless, stream of letters and characters with a few familiar words scattered within. He saw his name five times and naturally paid more attention to those areas. It didn't do any good. Everything seemed like a big confusing mess. It was clear that most of the data that was extracted from the human brain could not yet be translated into readable form. May be what Larry said was true. Some kind of encryption was being used by the brain itself. They were not being able to decode that encryption.

In the next two hours they turned over hundreds of more pages. They read stuff on varieties of topics, in tiny pieces. Only a few made sense.

*I hate space. But I have no choice. Mars, here I come.*

*I can't trust anybody. Danger everywhere.*

There was no date time associated with any of the data – at least not in a readable form. This meant they had no reasonable means to create a timeline of the events. Moreover, they found nothing about Wolf. Pete was somewhat disappointed. He knew this was going to be a long shot but deep inside he had a strong hope. The chip may actually have all the information he was looking for, but a quick finding was becoming an absurdity. Yet he decided to continue, at least for another few hours. He also tried to connect to Dan to discuss the progress. Strangely enough, Dan had suddenly become unreachable. Several calls went unanswered. Was he being too cautious? Not receiving calls on security reasons? Not impossible.

Time moved slowly through the night. Larisa and Jing Jing were tired and at some point lied down on the floor to rest. Pete noticed maneuvering the dummies were quite tiring and affected the brains in a way as if it was their natural body. He was alert, spirited. Michelle and Jason looked strong. Rico, with his grave, emotionless face, continued to analyze pages after pages, tirelessly. Pete had to admit, having him with them was a great thing. In the beginning they moved at the same pace but over time Pete slowed down, Rico didn't. Advantage of artificial intelligence.

Mila and Taz became tired of sitting idle. The ship flew on auto. There was not much to see with the exception of Jupiter, Mars and their visible moons. The billions of stars that lit the sky looked the same as they did from Earth and while presented them with a great view wasn't anything particularly interesting. When Pete bestowed him with the temporary Captainship of the Space Tiger about five hours ago, he was very excited though neither he nor Pete had any reason to believe that Taz would actually have to do anything. The ship was being operated by auto pilot and direction and speed were already set. Unless anything went drastically wrong, Taz had nothing to do besides keeping an eye. Even in case any mechanical problem popped up the automatic trouble shooting system could resolve most of them without any external interference. If for any reason it failed, the auto pilot would inform the captain and the controller.

Taz was really hoping for a smooth operation. He had ample training to handle and control a spaceship like this briefly, but in case of large scale problem he doubted if he would be able to manage. But never had he imagined that not happening anything could be so boring. Rest of the members of Space Tiger was still busy with the dummies. At some point they had shown some emotions but for the last several hours they looked pretty much dormant. He wondered what they were doing on Earth. He never thought this would turn into such a lengthy endeavor. He couldn't wait for them to come back safely.

"Being in a spaceship is really very boring," Mila yawned as she said it. "Let's go eat something. Sitting like this is going to make me rusty."

"I feel like having a special stew of rice and lintel that

my mom cooks sometimes," Taz said.

Mila chuckled. "Little nostalgic, huh! Yes, I ate that stew. Not bad. Is your mom a good cook?"

"Not good, great! She cooks everything I like."

"My mom doesn't like to cook at all," Mila said, unmindfully. "She is very independent minded. Dad begged her to come to Mars. She wouldn't. Instead, she wanted a divorce. Even I pleaded not to break up the family. She didn't care."

"What kind of person is your dad?"

"Usually very kind hearted but I have seen his tough side too. There are some things where he would not give in, especially anything related to City of Mars. That's his life."

"Would your dad go back to Earth ever again?"

"Why would he? He has everything right here. What do you want to eat? Let's see if I can make something."

"I'll eat whatever you make. Even a simple sandwich would do."

Mila rolled her eyes. "Why, were you expecting anything else?"

Taz chuckled. "I really like the way you talk."

Mila grinned. This boy was really naive.

# Chapter 18

Pete hadn't even noticed when the dawn started to break. Several hours had just flown by as they continued to browse through his father's memory. After struggling to stay awake for a while, finally Michelle had given up to tiredness. Jason proved to be too determined. His eyes were red for lack of sleep but he still remained awake. Rico didn't need sleep or any form of rest. He continued to look through pages after pages, desperately trying to get through as much information as he possibly could in the hope of finding some useful data. Pete was quite tired too. But he had no other option but to keep going. He tried to keep a keen eye on the text and an active mind to help Rico in the analysis. The only other human who didn't look tired at all was Larry, who kept mostly quiet but observant.

Finally, after hours later, they did get some reward for their persistence. They must have had gone through a few thousand memory pages when, for the first time, they saw the type of information they were looking for.

*I must find the probe. Mars…Mars…Mars…*

In a page filled with random meaningless

combination of letters these words just glowed like burning stars.

Larry looked alert as he stood with his back straightened. "This is exactly what we are looking for. Let's see if we find anything else."

Pete had his hopes up as well. This was a good start but he needed more. However, soon his hopes turned into disappointment. There was nothing else in the next few pages that even remotely had anything to do with Mars. There were a few known words here and there but meant nothing to them in the current context.

Again, they went back to their monotonous routine – looking through pages after pages…words after words… meaningless … worthless… Pete didn't even notice exactly when it started to happen…but for some strange reason the weird series of words started to make sense to him. After couple of hundred pages since the statement about the probe, he stumbled on a paragraph that at first looked like a series of totally garbled words but when he focused almost intuitively the words got rearranged in his mind:

> *They are very powerful. We have*
> *to stop them. But I don't know who*
> *they are. I hate my job."*

Larry noticed him looking at the screen keenly. He turned at him curiously. "Can you read anything in this page? I can't."

"Neither can I," Rico said. "Can you, Pete?"

Pete was thinking fast. Larry had mentioned that if there was a genetic relationship it could be easier to read encrypted material. But he hadn't really experienced that all through the night. Why suddenly now? Could it be that there was a threshold before the mechanism kicked in? Because not only that particular paragraph, now he could actually read most part of the page. Texts that looked worthless before made total sense now. But he wondered whether he should be sharing this information with Larry. Without his help they wouldn't be able to come this far, but at some point Larry's responsibility had to stop. He wished he had a chance to speak to Dan. Unfortunately, all his attempts to contact him failed. Dan didn't call him back either. This wasn't normal. Pete decided to ignore the question for the time being.

"What happened to Dan? Why is he so quiet suddenly?" He said, looking at Larry first and then at Rico. "Can you try to contact him, please?"

"I'll try," Rico said.

"You can read the content, right?" Larry wasn't ready to get distracted.

Pete was alarmed. Why was Larry so eager to know?

"No, Not really. I just thought I saw something there. Wrong. I couldn't make anything out of it."

Pete moved ahead. He still couldn't understand majority of the stuff that was shown but some of it he could. There was some information about Robert going to the Mars. There was also mention of Gary. He had received his father in Mars.

"Did you find anything in this page?" Larry demanded.

Pete was starting to get worried. Dan trusted Larry but how much?

Rico shook his head. "Pete, I can't connect to Dan. He is not picking up his phone."

Pete didn't like it at all. Something was wrong. But he didn't want to stop at this point. He still had some time in hand and he needed to explore the information as much as he could. He did not yet have what he was looking for. Dan must have had some reason to become unreachable for the time being. He decided to ignore Larry again and turned to next page. Possibly Larry was just too eager to help and Pete was being a little too paranoid. He didn't have time to worry about Larry now. There were still several questions he needed answer to. What was in that probe? Was there any connection between Wolf and his father? Who was Wolf?

He didn't have to wait too long. After a few more

pages something else popped up:

> *I do not know him. Nobody does.*
> *But I must find him. City of Mars*
> *is a small place. I'll find him.*

A little later:

> *What is in that probe? Why*
> *is it so important?*

Further down the pages:

> *Shrouded in beauty and love,*
> *here are my blessings that I leave for thee.*

Pete knew he was the only one who read that last statement because nobody else paid any attention to it. He tried to pretend as if he hadn't seen anything of importance, but that wasn't enough to fool Larry, who had been observing him with hawk eyes. "Did you see anything there?" he impatiently asked. "I think you did. Tell me the truth. You looked little longer at that section. What did you see? Why aren't you answering me?"

Before Pete could figure out a way to handle Larry,

he saw a pair of headlights approaching the house. It was a black, bullet proof car – a familiar model used by the VIPs. Expensive stuff but provided much higher degree of safety. Larry had seen the car too. He rushed to the window. "He found us, damn!"

He abruptly turned around and came rushing at Pete. Rico tried to stop him but he sent Rico in the air with a strong front kick. Rico took no time to jump back onto his feet, but Larry had already reached Pete. He threw a punch at Pete, targeting his lower abdomen. Suspicious and cautious, Pete was almost prepared for something like this. He moved back quickly to avoid the blow. Undeterred by the miss, Larry threw couple of quick kicks followed by a short flying kick. Pete blocked the first two with his hands and jumped further back out of Larry's range to avoid the deadly flying kick. Larry hit the wall and crashed part of it. In this commotion the sleeping members had woken up.

"What's going on?" Larisa screamed, startled.

Michelle was quick to act. She grabbed Larisa and Jing Jing and moved away from Larry and Pete.

"Pick up the reader and the chip, Rico," Pete instructed. "Everybody get out of here."

By the corner of his eyes he saw Dan stepping out of the car. He wasn't sure what was going on, but he was thankful to see him (Dan). Hopefully he came prepared. Pete brought back his attention to Larry, who had just recovered from the mishap with the wall and was looking at him with scorching eyes.

Dan heard something coming from inside the house and instantly knew not all was right. He took out his hand gun and carefully advanced to the front door. He got a glimpse of the basement through the window but could barely make out anything. The light was too dim and the glass was dusty. He carefully pushed the door open and stepped inside.

Rico went to get the reader without wasting any time but Larry was quick. He ignored Pete and came after him. With a strong kick on the chest he threw Rico on the ground and grabbed the reader. Pete came forward in Rico's help. He hit Larry on the neck with a strong round kick. Larry didn't see it coming until very late; he tried to move away but could not fully avoid it. The reader got thrown off of his hand. Jason was trying to pick it up, but before he could do so a small weapon came out in Larry's hand. A Laser gun.

"He has a laser gun!" Larisa shouted, warning everybody.

They tried to jump out of Larry's reach. But Larry didn't try to hit them. He blew off the reader in one direct shot. Pete saw a tiny opportunity and threw a flying kick hitting him on the back. The gun flew from Larry's hand and dropped on the floor. Larry didn't even try to pick it up. He ran to the stairs. Dan was coming down the stairs carefully. Larry pushed him away and ran out of the door. He climbed into his car and was gone in a blink.

Everything happened so quickly that it took them several moments to settle down. Dan's words brought everybody back to reality. "I was suspecting something like this," he said to Pete. "I have been trying to connect to you all night. He must have used a message scrambler. I was starting to get really worried."

Pete was surprised. "I thought Larry was your friend?"

Dan smiled. "Do you think he was Larry?"

"Who was he? He looked exactly like Larry."

"Don't know who he was, but he wasn't Larry. Somebody was using a dummy replica of Larry. Now the question is – where is Larry? Once you guys got out of the building, Larry followed you as well. They must have been waiting for him on the way. I hope he is okay."

Pete looked grave. "Who are they? Do you have any idea?"

"I wish I did," Dan sounded unhappy. "They definitely know who I am and may even know what I am up to. There are moles all over the place now - in CIA, FBI, Homeland Security, and in BSD for sure. Anyway, did you have any luck?"

Everybody turned their heads at Pete. He shrugged. "Should we discuss this here? The guy who just fled might have implanted a transmitter here. I think the car would be safer."

They got out of the house and quickly climbed into Dan's car. Dan drove it into the main street. Pete tried his best to feed Dan and the rest of the team's curiosity without giving up all the information that he had gathered. He did mention that he was able to read some of the encrypted data. He had no clue how. It just happened. If the man didn't burn the chip, he (Pete) would have probably found out some useful information. As there was nothing else to do on Earth, they disconnected from their dummies. The dummies stayed in Dan's car. He would take care of them later.

After returning from the virtual operation, most of them felt slightly nauseous. It took them a little while before they started to feel normal. There was no time to waste. Pete quickly went back to his captain's role. Taz provided him a quick report. Wolf hadn't contacted. This was good news as he didn't want Wolf to know about their little adventure. Wolf might still find out. Whoever kidnapped Larry and disguised as him, could very well be Wolf's associates. There was little doubt that he had capable friends back on Earth.

Later, he sat with Michelle and Jason to analyze their exchange plan. The rest of the team was sent to their cabins to relax. Only Rico had stayed back. He asked and received Pete's approval to stay on the bridge. Pete had already stopped suspecting him of spying for Gary. He definitely had allegiance to Garry, but to Pete's knowledge, it was next to impossible to totally control a highly intelligent robot. On the other hand, Gary wouldn't have planned something sinister when his own daughter was in the ship.

At some point, their recent experience on Earth made way into their conversation.

"Around the end it appeared to me that you hit something," Michelle said. "Can you share that with us?"

Pete thought about it for a moment. He didn't say it to Dan in the car because he couldn't be totally sure about his identity. After returning, he contacted the controller and left a message for Dan. The security system that was built around the controllers was of very high quality. Nobody had ever been able to break that system. He put his trust in it. Once Dan received that message and sent a note back to him, he would be sure about Dan's identity. He hadn't received anything from Dan yet.

Pete wondered whether he should share his findings with the team yet. The piece of information that Michelle was referring to, looked more like a riddle with some sort of vague meaning, though, he had this feeling that it was important. Riddle or not, he felt an urgency to know what it meant.

"I saw something – like a puzzle," Pete said. "I don't know what it means. I guess you guys didn't see it."

"Nope," Michelle said. "I saw only worthless words, but you lit up. You probably didn't know that. It was obvious that you found something."

"What is that puzzle?" Jason asked.

Pete revealed it.

*Shrouded in beauty and love,*

*here are my blessings that I leave for thee.*

Nobody spoke for a few moments as they tried to solve it. Even Rico went into deep thought. He was probably checking into the data banks of any system that he had access to. If he didn't find anything anywhere, then he would go into analysis mode.

After several minutes Michelle gave up with a shrug. "It seems that your father had hidden the probe somewhere. If we can solve this puzzle, we would probably know the location of it. I am starting to believe, your dad might have had some sort of trouble with Wolf after all."

"Clearly, dad worked for American secret services," Pete thoughtfully said. "Could be CIA, FBI or something like that. This is what I think might have happened. Wolf secretly brought some stuff to Mars from Earth. Dad was sent to find Wolf. Something had happened here. Wolf escaped. Dad returned to Earth. Wolf never returned. At least not that we know of. Now the question is what happened on Mars? If I had a little more time I could have found it. I was starting to see things. The words that had no meaning before suddenly started to make sense. It was almost like they were in disguise and I could simply see through their disguises. Anyway, that discussion is useless now. The data chip has been destroyed. I don't think we'll be able to go anywhere near dad again. They must have put heavier security in place by now. Larry's identity must have gotten revealed too."

This was when he received Dan's message, finally. Dan sent an acknowledgement. Pete informed him about the puzzle.

"The probe is not in Mars," Rico said, after several minutes. "Robert could have sent it anywhere in the space. Where should we look for it in this vast space?"

"Good point," Pete said. "The question is would he send it too far risking losing it, or would he send it nearby so that he could recover it at an opportune time. Of course, he had to make sure that the location was not too obvious. He took it quite seriously. Even in his mind he stored the information in a riddle form – possibly as a precaution, just in case something happened to him and he was frozen."

"He was a remarkable man!" Jason said, respectfully.

"Yep! James bond 007," Pete quipped.

Michelle smiled. "Like father like son. Dashing!"

There was a clear touch of admiration in her voice, an obvious fondness, nobody would have missed it. Pete almost instinctively looked at Jason, which he regretted moments later. Jason tried his best to pretend as if he cared little about it, but the deep shadow that anchored over his face gave it all away. He had strong, genuine love for Michelle. Pete knew that. Such feelings were bound to produce some sensitivity – perhaps for all the good reasons. Pete took his eyes of him and simply walked away mumbling something about an important task.

After couple of hours, the whole team gathered in the bridge. The excitement and anxiety, both were hard to hide. The exchange would take place in just a few hours. None of them had any idea how Wolf was planning to do this. Pete noticed the four youngsters were equally excited and restless. This was natural, he admitted. At that age, it was hard to see the risk and everything looked exciting. At twenty two, he felt like a senior. Being the captain of a large ship with so much responsibility wasn't easy! Sometimes even he had difficulty coping with it.

Pete asked the team to gather at the center and

briefed them about what could be coming next. He also shared the riddle with all of them. He needed all the minds working on it. There was no telling who would come up with the answer.

# Chapter 19

Wolf contacted several hours later than expected. Pete was starting to get a little worried, wondering if Wolf had changed his mind. But his fear proved to be unfounded. Wolf was still interested in moving on with the hostage exchange, but he added a new condition. Pete won't go alone. He would have to take Michelle with him. Two for two. Pete was mad.

"Why are you pulling Michelle into this?" He protested.

Wolf broke into laughter. "You are a smart guy. You know why I need her. She would be my trump card. With her in the ship, you won't act, let's say, irresponsibly."

"I love my life. I'll behave, I promise. You have nothing to worry about. Just leave her alone."

"Do you want President's daughter back or not?" Wolf teased.

Pete was disappointed. This guy knew his game. Pete had very little choice but to comply. He took a deep breath. "How do you want to do the exchange?"

"I want to make it simple," Wolf said. "I'll send the tourists in a capsule. Once they reach your spaceship, get them off the capsule, you and Michelle take their places, and fly back to my spaceship."

"Where is the twist?" Pete asked.

"There will be bombs attached to their bodies. Once you two reach my spaceship, I'll deactivate those. If anything goes wrong, you can imagine how it would turn out."

"This is not acceptable," Pete said. "What guarantee is there that you won't blow them off?"

"No guarantees," Wolf said. "I don't think you have any other choice but to trust me."

Pete laughed. "You think you are too smart? I have very high power laser cannons in my spaceship. Those will be trained on yours. You try anything stupid your ship will get roasted."

"In that case, we are on the level ground," Wolf said, lightly. "I love my life too. I also don't like to blow anybody off, not unless I run out of choices. I am a peaceful man. Let's do this peacefully."

Pete didn't trust Wolf. He couldn't be sure what was Wolf planning to do. He hadn't yet answered the vital question, why he needed Pete? "When do you want to do the exchange?" He tried to stay calm.

"I am going to send you my coordinates in a few moments. Be there in exactly half an hour."

Wolf disconnected. Pete received the coordinates and entered it in the Deep Space Navigation System (DSNS).

Wolf wasn't too far. It would take Space Tiger no more than twenty minutes to cover the distance. This meant they had a little time to adjust their plan. However, with the hostages wrapped with bombs, it didn't seem like a good idea to try anything at all. Pete knew he had to play his hand very carefully. Until he had a clear idea how important he was to Wolf, he couldn't be sure how much risk he could take. He had no problem risking his own life, but the last thing he wanted was to put his crews into unnecessary danger.

Jason had been quiet for a while, but when he finally broke his silence it was not something that Pete wanted to deal with. He outright refused to let Michelle go into this danger. Pete understood his concern, but at the same time he knew he had no way to avoid this. Instead of getting into direct conflict with Jason, he cleverly allowed Michelle to take care of it. Michelle took Jason away from the bridge. Everybody knew Jason would eventually calm down.

After a short team meeting it was decided that for the time being, all plans were off the table. Once the hostage exchange completed successfully, and the bombs were inactivated, only then they would even consider doing anything. Also, it was decided that the hostages would be received in the cargo section. If for any reason Wolf triggered the bombs, only one part of the spaceship would possibly bear some damage. That would not stop it from functioning. In case the damage was more than expected, it could be flown to Mars for repair. Before the exchange, Pete had a routine work to complete. He made Jason the interim Captain. Taz will be at the navigation. Larisa and Jing Jing would stay close, ready to help whoever needed it. Rico and Mila had no particular responsibility, but they were asked to stay on the bridge and work with Jason. Mila looked pretty unhappy, possibly mad.

"Mila, do you want to say something?" Pete gave her an opportunity to vent out.

"I think you are doing a big mistake," Mila grumbled. "You should not do this exchange. This bad ass had been causing lot of trouble in Mars for many years. We know where he would be. There is no reason to exchange. Let's attack his spaceship, rescue the two tourists, and blow his head off."

"We are not going to do any such thing," Rico quickly said, apologetically. "Let's not forget, Pete is the captain. We must comply with his instructions."

"Captain my foot!" Mila snapped.

There was a series of chuckles. Pete had difficulty swallowing the bubbling laughter. This girl had a mind of her own. "Listen," He said, "if Wolf was alone then we could try things like that. But the two tourists are in his spaceship. We can't do anything without first knowing where and how they are kept inside the spaceship. If we attack preemptively, not only we put them in serious danger, we actually put us and Space Tiger at risk too. So, let's not consider that. Instead, I want all of you to start working on the riddle. I have a strong feeling if we can find the answer to this riddle, we'll have the key to Wolf's secrets."

"Puzzle my foot!" Mila twisted her lips in disgust.

"Why don't you solve it then?" Taz dared to tease.

"Why aren't you doing it, genius?" Mila shot back.

Taz was quick to surrender. He wasn't going to get into trouble by pissing her off.


Pete showed up at the given coordination on time. There was no sign of the Dark Wolf. It couldn't be too far, Pete guessed. Perhaps Wolf was intentionally delaying, trying to make sure that he wasn't stepping into a trap laid by Pete.

Wolf contacted after about five long minutes. He informed that he was approaching Space Tiger and would stop about 7 to 8 thousand kilometers away. Few seconds later, the Dark Wolf showed up on the monitor like a small dot. It advanced another 1600 kilometers (1000 miles) or so before coming to a standstill at 7000 kilometers (~4500 miles) away. After a few moments, another tiny dot popped up on the screen. It was the capsule, Pete assumed. Wolf's voice became live on the radio. "I am sending the tourists.

No tricks. I don't want any trouble."

"Me neither," Pete responded. "Please have dinner ready. We are hungry." He noticed the environment inside the bridge had become very tense. Everybody looked immensely worried. He wanted to lighten up the situation a little bit. Nervous people could end up making bad choices. His remark brought out a few chuckles. Not too bad, Pete thought.

"Looks like you are in good spirit," Wolf said.

"I am trying. It's your party. You are not doing much to entertain us," Pete said. He noticed the second dot was approaching them rapidly.

"All the cannons are pointed at them," Michelle said. She had been pressing buttons on a key panel with utmost attention.

"I am controlling them," Jason said. He was standing before the monitor, watching the advancing dot with keen eyes. "I don't think he would try to do anything stupid."

They really hoped Wolf wouldn't. The bright dot had grown bigger to a point, where they could now see it through the windows. Taz moved the ship to an angle, so that the capsule can only enter the cargo space.

"There must be cameras in the capsule," Pete said. "Keep the ship standstill. Don't let him get concerned."

Taz was surprised to realize how calm he was. Here

they were in a situation that could blow up into a really dangerous way and he was at the control, handling the Space Tiger! He very carefully applied opposing forces to bring the ship to a standstill.

The capsule floated into the cargo space slowly and stopped slightly above the ground. The automatic door slid open and almost immediately climbed out the two tourists wrapped in special space suits. Once they removed their helmets, the sheer panic in their faces shook everybody in the bridge. The woman looked hysteric, while the man was terrified.

"My name is Mary Bird," the woman said, almost whispering. "He is my husband, James Bird."

"We know everything about you," Pete said, who went to receive them, alone.

"There are bombs tied to our bodies," James said.

"I know," Pete said. "Please wait here. The bombs will be disabled soon. Don't be afraid. Wolf kidnapped you because he wanted to get hold of me. Once I and my colleague reach his ship, he would disable your bombs."

"We couldn't see anything inside his ship," Pete hadn't asked but both of them spontaneously offered. "He kept us in a dark room. But he didn't torture us or anything."

Noticing the small bulges under their suits, Pete readily knew those weren't very powerful bombs. If blown up, those bombs weren't going to be able to damage the spaceship but would easily kill the tourists. He called Michelle to the cargo space. Just moments later, she walked in wrapped in a skin tight space suit.

"Ready?" Pete asked.

Michelle nodded silently. By watching her quiet face it was impossible to tell what was going on in her mind. Pete smiled trying to give her some strength. Michelle smiled back. Jason stood by her. He probably wanted to give her a hug but Michelle did not show any interest.

"Keep them here for now with the suit on," Pete said to Jason referring the tourists. "Once we reach there and the bombs are disabled, then take them inside."

"O.K., Pete," Jason said gravely, as always.

"Once we settle in the Dark Wolf, I'll try to contact you," Pete said, as he climbed into the capsule and took a seat. Michelle followed him and sat on a chair facing him. This was a large capsule with seating capacity for six people. The capsule door slid closed. Moments later it flew out of the open cargo door into the space. A mechanical voice spoke out.

"Thank you Pete, for keeping it peaceful," said Wolf.

Pete did not respond. There was no doubt this cabin had hidden cameras. He needed to act very normal, making sure that Wolf could not see how scared he was – inside.

"What do you think is going to happen once we go inside his spaceship?" Michelle asked, whispering.

"We'll see," Pete said. "I don't think anything bad would happen too soon."

"There got to be something really big behind all this."

"That's how it looks like. Who knows? Let's see if he reveals any secret."

"Why did he ask for me?" Michelle asked.

"Probably knows I have weakness for you. He is trying to use that. If you are with me, I'll act much more carefully."

Michelle blushed. "You should not talk like that."

"I know. I just felt like saying. I'll never do it again."

"You know if you really want me, I may not be able to resist it. You do know that, don't you?"

"I know. Sorry. I won't talk like that again. In this type of mission, a man's heart can become weak."

Michelle spoke after being silent for a long moment. "Jason is a wonderful person. I probably wouldn't have thought about anybody else if I didn't meet you. I feel guilty sometimes."

"Okay, let's not ever again talk about these things. We are there. I can see Dark Wolf."

It was a bright dot in the dark; quite obviously that

was the infamous Dark Wolf. Right at that moment, something strange struck their vision. Another smaller dot was rushing at Dark Wolf very rapidly.

"Pete! Pete!" They could hear Jason's panicked voice. "Mila took one of our capsules and went after the Dark Wolf."

"What? How? Where was Rico? What is she planning to do?" Pete became nervous. He shouldn't have trusted this girl. She could probably sacrifice her life for City of Mars.

"I don't know, but Rico went after her," Jason said, shaken.

There was very little chance of seeing Rico with bare eyes. Most probably he jumped wearing only a space suit. Smartmans were much more effective in space than humans were. They could travel in the space without a ship quite easily. Though they still had to wear a suit to maintain body pressure, otherwise they would get blown up.

"Wolf! Wolf! Can you hear me?" Pete shouted, hoping there was a transmitter inside the capsule.

"What the hell is happening?" Wolf sounded annoyed. "I can see a capsule rushing toward us. Who is in it? I have asked it to stop. If it doesn't stop, I'll blow it up."

"It's Mila, Gary's daughter," Pete said. "I had no idea she was planning something like this. Don't do anything stupid. There's no bomb in that capsule. You can easily avoid her."

"Why is this girl so crazy? The capsule is coming right toward my ship. What a pain!" Wolf gasped.

The next series of events happened very quickly. Mila set the direction of her capsule toward Dark Wolf and jumped out a few seconds before the possible impact. Her intention was simple. The capsule would burst after colliding with the ship. As a result, the ship could catch fire. There was little possibility of large scale damage. Wolf cleverly moved his ship out of the path of the capsule and allowed the tiny thing to pass by his ship safely and fly into the dark space beyond.

After jumping into the space, Mila was drifting away uncontrollably. Rico detected her and followed. Mila wasn't very surprised. She kind of knew Rico would come to her rescue. Rico caught her safely and brought her back to the Space Tiger without any further incident.

Pete sighed in relief. "That's it. She is never stepping into my ship again! How could she be so arrogant? She can't just do whatever comes to her mind."

Michelle relaxed into her seat. "She needs to learn anger management."

The capsule entered into the Dark Wolf through an open gate. Once the gate closed, the place flooded in artificial light. This was a capsule dock. The capsule slowed down and parked in its designated spot, next to another one. The automatic door slid open. A robot came forward to greet them. "Come with me please."

They had to walk through a full body scanner. They were led through a narrow corridor to the bridge, which was relatively small, old, sign of aging everywhere. Wolf was sitting in the Captain's seat, wearing his usual wolf's mask. He smiled and shook hands. "It is an honor to have you in my spaceship, Pete. How is your shoulder?"

"It's healing. I had to take some strong medication. But let's take care of the business first," Pete anxiously said. "Please deactivate the bombs."

"Of course," Wolf gave him a rectangular object that looked like a controller. A red diode glowed strongly. There were several buttons. "The cancel button would disable it," Wolf said. "The bombs are tied with straps. Just ask them to unstrap and throw them out, problem solved. Cheap stuff."

Before pressing the button, Pete looked at Wolf one more time. Was he setting him up? Wolf shook his head. "I maybe a bad guy, but I do know what is good for me. Press with confidence."

Pete pressed the cancel button. The red light on the controller turned into green. Wolf gave him a radio. "It's connected. Just speak. They'll hear you."

Pete instructed Jason to throw away the bombs and

provide the tourists a cabin to rest.

Wolf laughed in relief. "Thanks God, this part went very well. I was really worried. You are too smart. Just couldn't be sure what you might do. We'll have to fight one more time. You are a good fighter. Let's go, eat dinner. There is a lady with us. We need to show her due respect."

"Dinner?" Pete looked at him suspiciously.

"Exactly what you asked for," Wolf broke into laughter. It was clear he was enjoying the whole situation very much.

# Chapter 20

Wolf arranged for a grand dinner. He actually had a dining room with a proper wooden table. The table was filled with delicious food – from roasted chicken to barbecued pork, mashed potato to baked cheese biscuits. Pete and Michelle looked stunned for a few long moments. Having this kind of food in a spaceship was like dream. No doubt, Wolf got his food supplies from Mars. There were several animal farms operating in Mars inside various resorts. They had come up with ways to keep some animals like chicken and pigs within very small spaces. Supplies of some other stuff also came regularly from Earth. Wolf chuckled delightfully at their amazement.

The food tasted quite good. None of them were really hungry but still decided to eat. If Wolf had gone through the difficulties to arrange such a grand dinner, it would be unfair not to accept it. Wolf was a big eater. He gorged on the food only occasionally taking time to check on his guests. There was very little conversation. With mouth full of food, it would have been hard for Wolf to speak anyway. Two Smartmans stood by the table, offering to serve every few minutes. Pete kept his ears trained outside to pick up any sound from walking or chatting to determine how many others – human or Smartmans – were in the ship. He heard nothing. Outside the dining room, the only sound that he heard was a humming from the engine.

Pete thought Wolf would want to talk after the dinner, but apparently that wasn't how Wolf had planned. He sent them to their respective cabins located next to each other one floor below the bridge. The two Smartmans escorted them to their cabins and stayed nearby. Wolf surely wasn't taking any chances. Both of the guards were armed with strong laser guns.

Half an hour later he called only Pete in the bridge. Pete was waiting for this. He was dying to know the truth. One of the Smartman guided him to the bridge, where Wolf met him. There were a few small windows allowing a glimpse of the dark space outside. Pete couldn't be sure, but he believed the spaceship was most probably standing still. Which meant, Space Tiger wasn't moving either. He tried to connect to Space Tiger from his cabin but did not succeed. Wolf didn't take his phone away but disabled all communication channels.

Wolf was relaxing in a cushioned seat. He asked Pete to take a seat next to him on a large, cushioned sofa. Pete took a deep breath and complied. Wolf looked very in control, calm. He had seen Pete fight. How could he be so calm? Pete wondered. Nobody was pointing a gun at him.

Wolf looked unarmed as well. Perhaps he was rooting on the fact that Pete wouldn't do anything foolish before the mystery was revealed. And of course the trump card – Michelle, who was staying in her cabin guarded by a Smartman. Pete noticed two other Smartmans were sitting behind the control, operating the ship.

"How many men do you have in the ship?" Pete lightly asked, almost as a leading question to break the ice.

"There are some more Smartmans," Wolf answered smilingly. "No, there are no other humans beside me, if you consider me one."

Pete couldn't figure out if there was any touch of sadness in his tone. Even if there was, he wouldn't have cared much. This man was not by any means a good man. He gave an impression to be a calm, calculative, and criminally active person. There was no doubt he had brought Pete here for a very specific reason. Pete could barely wait to know what it was. However, he knew Wolf wasn't going to reveal the mystery too quickly, if ever.

Wolf went to business without wasting much time. "I know you have no idea why you are here. You shouldn't. Let me also confess, I am not about to tell you everything. And finally, please don't try anything silly. The girl is in my hand."

Pete smiled. "A man of your size is scared of me, I am honored."

"You are a great fighter. At the same time, I am not as young either. Anyway, let me tell you why you are here. I am looking for a probe. I thought if I could capture you, I would be able to find it relatively easily."

"What probe? I know nothing about any probe," Pete pretended to be surprised.

"You didn't but now you do. Do you remember analyzing the copy of your dad's brain in a basement in New York City?"

"So it was you? I thought it was one of your associates on Earth. Where is Larry? Is he okay?"

"He is just fine. He slept for a little bit."

"You do have accomplices on Earth, don't you? You can't be all by yourself."

"Do you really need to know? Why do you want to get into unnecessary trouble? I admit I have heard a lot of good things about you. I am really happy to meet you. Honestly, I don't want to put you into any kind of danger. Just give me what I am looking for, you go in your way, I go mine."

"Great idea! But what is it that you want? Don't tell me it's about some probe."

"I need the location of the probe."

"How would I know? We didn't get anything last night. Remember?"

"I don't believe that. Around the end of our session, you looked as if you could read the encryption. May be not everything, but some of it. I have seen it happening several times before. I know the look. I believe you know something that may be of use to me."

"You are wrong. I could have, if I got more time. You destroyed the memory chip. If you needed the information so badly, why destroy it?"

"Let's just say, there are earthlings who I must keep happy. They didn't want me to leave it in your hand."

There was a brief silence. Both looked at each other as if measuring up the other person. A storm of thoughts blew through Pete's mind. Though Wolf hadn't given up many details, he could sort of figure it out. Clearly Wolf and his father were acquainted. There was something in the probe – something very important. His father was sent to get it away from Wolf. Whatever happened at the end, his father sent it somewhere in the space, possibly to hide it from Wolf.

Would it be a good idea to let Wolf know about the riddle? Pete wondered. He was considering all kind of possibilities. What if Wolf knew the answer? What would he do? Would he really allow them to leave as he went on to his own way? What were his orders? If he didn't know the answer of the riddle that probably would be safer, Pete concluded. Because then, he wouldn't want to harm Pete, not until he had the answer. Not knowing who his bosses were, it was difficult to predict what they wanted him to do. Nevertheless, Pete wanted to take the best decision under the existing circumstances. There was no room for errors. It wasn't just his life that depended on his decision, but his crews and the ship's fate as well.

"Just tell me what you know. I won't harm you," Wolf said. "That won't be good for me either. You are a superstar of Bureau of Space Detectives. Dan has kept the organization functioning basically showing you. If anything happens to you, a lot of people on Earth will be in trouble. So you have nothing to worry. Remember one thing, in space, I do not always allow my bosses to control me."

Pete decided to reveal the riddle. Not that he trusted Wolf, but at this point that seemed like the only way to get out of this jeopardy. "I did get something, like a riddle. I don't know the answer. May be you would. *Shrouded in beauty and motherly love, here are my blessings that I leave to thee.* Do you have any idea what it means?"

Wolf repeated it once. He shook his head thoughtfully. "Nothing else?"

"No. I probably would have found more if you hadn't burnt the thing. I don't think asking the Library of Science for another copy is an option."

"Not unless you want to end up in a jail," Wolf chuckled. "We had been looking for someone like Larry for long time. Don't know how Dan found him. Anyway, after that incident all access to the Frozens has been closed for indefinite period. I could present you as a hostage and demand a copy of your father's brain, but there's no immediate need for such drama right now. I also doubt if that would work. You are valuable to BSD, but the US government is a different organization and may not be that willing. Let me think about the riddle first. Thanks for sharing it. That was the right thing to do. If I can't find the answer, then I'll have to come up with another action plan. Sorry to put you and the girl through all this, but I must find the probe."

Wolf sent Pete to his cabin. Before entering the cabin Pete knocked on Michelle's door but didn't get any answer. He looked at the guard, who simply nodded as if to say she was inside. Pete went into his cabin and tried to rest. He felt a sudden kick of anxiety. He couldn't feel safe putting his and Michelle's fate in Wolf's hand.

After bringing Mila back from space in one piece, Rico scolded her mercilessly. He even called Gary up and let him know. Mila refused to talk to her father. She went in her cabin and kept the door locked until Rico calmed down. As the in-charge captain of the ship, Jason had some responsibility too. He put restrictions on Mila. She wouldn't be permitted to go near any control panel. The capsule was salvaged but Mila had no access to it anymore. Rico was asked to keep a close eye on her. She could come to the bridge but must sit at the back.

Jason had never thought that Mila could end up doing something so reckless. He was feeling really down. He was the in-charge Captain of the spaceship. He must take full responsibility. He had been a complete failure. Good thing it didn't end up in a disaster. If Wolf had lost his nerve and read the situation differently, it could easily turn into a full scale battle. Fortunately, things ended peacefully and nobody got hurt. Most of all, the tourists were both safe and sound. Gary sent a spaceship to take them back to Mars. Later, they would take one of the passenger spaceships and return to Earth. That ship should reach soon. Interestingly, Dark Wolf didn't move even an inch since the exchange, which was almost couple of days ago as per Earth time. There was no way to know what was Wolf up to. He tried to connect to Pete and Michelle, but had no luck. He also tried to contact Wolf, but got no response either.

While very worried about Pete and Michelle, he knew what he had to do. He would follow Dark Wolf to hell, if he had to. He only hoped he could pass the two tourists before Dark Wolf got going. Things had been kind of stressful on board of Space Tiger. Taz, Larisa and Jing Jing stayed with him in the bridge most of the time, primarily keeping busy trying to solve the riddle. They had no luck yet. Mila barely came out of her cabin.

On day three, Jason had just enough. He felt like moving close to Dark Wolf. At least that would force Wolf to respond. Only if he knew what was going on inside Dark Wolf. Were Pete and Michelle safe? Did Wolf hurt them? Why was he keeping them hostage? Why wasn't he going anywhere? Should he try to rescue his colleagues? He couldn't be sure what to do and decided to wait. The last thing he wanted was to do something foolish and put everybody in danger.

The trainees had been noticing Jason closely. He was tense but held up quite well. On the third day, when he started to pace up and down the bridge relentlessly, they realized he needed some support. Larisa came ahead to offer some counseling. "Don't worry so much. Wolf won't hurt them. He is a smart guy. He knows what is bad for him."

Jing Jing agreed. "Dan would mess him up, and his bosses – whoever they are."

"Does Dan have lot of power?" Taz asked.

"There are more than hundred countries involved in

BSD. If Dan wants, he can do a lot of things," Larisa said.

Jason didn't bet on that. Out of hundred plus members only a handful paid the bills. The rest simply wanted to rip off the benefits. Dan still had some authority, but he wasn't sure if that was enough to intimidate Wolf or his so called bosses on Earth.

Several hours later, Mila joined them in the bridge. Rico escorted her and stayed within arm's length. She took a seat at the back of the bridge as instructed. Taz greeted her and tried to start a conversation. She outright ignored him and took out a small reader from her pocket and started to read something. This was embarrassing, Taz had to admit.

# Chapter 21

Pete wasn't sure exactly how long he had been lying down. Two days had passed since they had stepped into Wolf's spaceship. After the meeting with Wolf in the bridge, he had spent most of the time in his cabin. Wolf hadn't asked for him or visited him. It was almost like he had no need for Pete any more. The two guards stayed outside their cabins around the clock. Food was brought to them by another Smartman. They were allowed to eat together but were asked to stay in their own cabins unless told otherwise. Pete had been spending most of his time either reading or napping. There was a television and plenty of stored movies and shows, but he wasn't in the mode. He wondered how Michele was spending her time. Most of all, what was Wolf up to? The spaceship hadn't moved yet. What was he waiting for?

Staring at the ceiling he was about to doze off again, when the door opened slightly and a light footstep walked in. The lights inside had been dimmed but he could still clearly see Michelle, who walked to his bed and stood quietly. He could smell the familiar charming odor of her perfume. Not sure exactly what happened to him, but he did something that he hadn't done before. He held her hand. This felt wrong but he couldn't undo this. He hoped vaguely that Michelle would move away and this intimacy would be broken. Michelle didn't. She stood silently as their hands felt the warmth of each other for a few long moments.

"How did you get here?" Pete asked.

"The guards didn't stop me," Michelle said. "I was feeling really down. What do you think Wolf is planning to do? It has been more than two days and nothing has happened. I don't think we are even moving."

Pete shrugged. "We are not. After the dinner on first day, we met. I gave him the riddle. May be he is trying to solve it."

"Did you get anything from him?"

"Nope. He didn't reveal much," Pete felt Michelle was sweating under his hand but she made no attempt to take her hands away, as if none of them wanted to lose in this game.

"I have a bad feeling," Michelle muttered.

"Don't be afraid. Nothing bad will happen," Pete pressed her hand lightly and let it go. He was starting to feel guilty.

Michelle sat by his bed. "Everything is so quiet. It feels weird."

"Tell me about it," Pete chuckled. She was right. Beside a humming noise from the engine everything else was so calm and quiet that it almost felt like a ghost town.

Michelle stayed for half an hour. They spoke about Space Tiger and the team members they left behind. Both wondered how Jason was handling the pressure. What was *trouble girl* Mila doing? And the trainees – how were they coping up with all this suspense?

Two hours later, the quietness of the Dark Wolf was broken by Wolf's deep voice on the microphone. "Good news! Pete, Michelle, you are no longer welcome in my spaceship. Two of my Smartmans would help you into a capsule. That would take you back to the Space Tiger."

Surprised, Pete and Michelle came out in the corridor. They exchanged stares, not sure how to take this new development. What was Wolf up to now? Why the sudden change of mind? Did he solve the riddle? Was that why he had no use for them anymore? Pete called out for Wolf several times but got no response. "He is ignoring me," Pete muttered.

The two Smartman guards escorted them to the capsule dock. Pete was clearly disappointed. He had high hopes of finding out some details from Wolf. So much for that. At least they were returning unharmed. That was something to be happy for. The good part was if Wolf had found the location of the probe, Pete could simply follow him to it. Though, he admitted, it was too much to expect that Wolf would be so naïve not to see that possibility. He must have already made a plan to tackle that.

"Step in," one of the Smartmans pointed at a capsule and commanded.

Pete had a faint hope that Wolf would come to see them off. But he wasn't to be seen anywhere. Pete allowed Michelle to climb in first and followed her into the capsule. He hesitated for a moment, but at the end sat beside Michelle, with their hands touching. Michelle looked little surprised but didn't move away. Deep inside Pete felt guilty again, but then he knew once they returned to Space Tiger everything would go back to the usual way. He just couldn't let go this rare opportunity of intimacy. The capsule door closed automatically. Seconds later, the capsule emerged from the spaceship and headed into the dark. Looking out of the windows they could see the lights of Dark Wolf moving away at a very fast pace. Pete did a mental calculation. At the speed their capsule was moving, it shouldn't take more than a few minutes to reach Space Tiger.

"Do you think they know that we are coming back?" Michelle sounded doubtful.

"It is a little suspicious," Pete admitted. "I am not sure why Wolf suddenly turned so quiet."

Dark Wolf had now totally disappeared from their view. They expected to see the Space Tiger soon. As

Michelle eagerly looked out to pick up the lights of their spaceship, Pete diverted his attention to inside the capsule. This was a usual looking capsule with a control panel and a large wall monitor located at one side. This type of capsules could be controlled from inside or from a mother ship. Pete walked up to the screen and pressed a few buttons. Nothing happened. He readily knew they did not have the control of the capsule. It was locked. Somebody was controlling it from outside, must be Wolf or one of his Smartmans.

"Are we going in the right direction?" Michelle said, concerned.

"If we did we should have seen Space Tiger by now," Pate said. He tried the onboard radio to connect to his spaceship. No luck. Wolf had all systems locked.

"What is he trying to do?" Michelle guessed it but wanted Pete to confirm her suspicion.

"Exactly what you are thinking," Pete sighed in despair. This was what he was afraid of. "He sent us in the opposite direction and went off in his way. He must have sent a note to the Space Tiger, so that they come looking for us. This buys him some time to disappear. Simple plan but effective."

"Do you really think he informed Jason?" Michelle sounded unsure.

"I hope so," Pete tried to be positive. "He is a bad

ass, but is he that bad to throw us into the space like this?"

"I hope not," Michelle dryly said. She could almost see them starving to death in this small cabin, drifting away aimlessly into the endless space.

Pete read her mind. "Don't panic. Jason is coming for us. Today or tomorrow he'll find us."

Michelle took a deep breath. "Do you really believe that?"

"I do, sort of. I am afraid Wolf might have given Jason a wrong direction too. Which means, it is going to be much longer than a day or two before we see Space Tiger," Pete laid it off.

"If we drift away too far, how will they find us?"

"Good question. If they don't find us, you are doomed. You'll be with me forever," Pete joked.

"Don't joke. I am not in the mood. Can we really get lost in the space?" Michelle asked.

"You know the answer. It could be fun, no? But what would we eat? There's no food here. We can't control this thing. Starving to death can't be fun."

"Can you stop kidding please?" Michelle snapped.

"Sorry. I am just trying to lighten things up a little," Pete said. He gave her a light hug. "Don't worry. We'll find a way out. I believe Wolf have set up a timer. Once the time is over, we'll get control of this capsule and fly toward Mars.

Even if we can't find the Space Tiger, we'll still get to Mars. It'll take us longer but we'll get there. I mean, think about this, if he really wanted to harm us, he could have done that long ago. There was no need to sacrifice a good capsule."

Michelle didn't say anything. She kept staring outside. Pete started to feel a little worried as well but tried not to show that. He didn't know Wolf very well. Was it possible he was being too optimistic? Hopefully not. He tried not to think about the dreadful possibility of starving to death.

Space Tiger found them after two days. Pete was right about Wolf, to his relief. After twenty four hours, they got control of the capsule. They had to wait another twelve hours to get control of the radio. Finally, when they parked the capsule inside the Space Tiger and stepped out of it, Pete let out a deep sigh. It was good to be back; especially bringing Michelle back in one piece was a great relief. Wolf went away, that was okay. If they found the answer to the riddle, they could still catch up with him, assuming he was flying toward the location of the probe. Dark Wolf was an old spaceship. Despite the fact that Wolf had updated it considerably, it was still nowhere near as powerful as Space Tiger was. But the question was would they be able to figure out the riddle before it was too late? Or was it already late? Perhaps Wolf had already found what he was looking for and disappeared with it, not to be found ever again.

Pete gathered the whole team in the bridge soon after returning to the spaceship. A lot had happened and he felt there was a need for briefing. Jason looked happy to be relieved of his responsibility as a captain. He must have said sorry ten times to Pete and Michelle for Mila's action. Pete tried his best to comfort him and to bring back his confidence, but he realized with someone like Jason it wasn't going to happen too quickly. He provided the team a brief description of what happened in Dark Wolf. Next he went on to describe his immediate plan – which was practically nothing but to return to Mars.

"So, we won't be able to catch Wolf?" Rico sounded unhappy.

"We can still catch him if we can find the answer of the riddle soon enough," Pete tried to sound hopeful. "One thing we definitely know, the riddle is talking about a location. That can be a planet, a star or just space. In all likelihood, that can be the location where the probe is, the probe that Wolf is looking for. I am certain that's where he is heading to. So, let's all think about it once more. This can't be so difficult!"

"Aren't you the captain of the ship, the great Pete?" Mila mocked. "Why can't you solve it? What kind of detective are you?"

Pete chuckled. Why was this girl always so cranky? Not even sparing the Captain from her wrath! "Listen young lady, you have already caused a lot of trouble," he tried to sound as tough as he could without sounding mean. "We could have all died by now. I am the Captain of this ship, you said that right. You need to learn to show respect to me. It is part of your training."

"I didn't come here for training. I came here to kill that bastard Wolf. He escaped because of you. Damn!" Mila muttered grudgingly.

Taz raised his hand. "Can I say something?"

"Watch it!" Mila warned.

"She said she knows the answer," Taz murmured.

All the eyes turned at Mila. "Really?" Rico sounded unconvinced.

"What is so difficult about it?" Mila impatiently said. "Everybody should know this. No wonder Wolf figured it out so quickly."

"If you have the answer, why aren't you sharing it?" Michelle softly said. "Don't you want to catch Wolf?"

"You don't want to catch him. You just want to know what he is running after," Mila angrily said. "I'll take care of him. I don't need your help."

It wasn't too long before Mila revealed the answer. Pete had to give his word of honor that he would go after

Wolf, and there was no other alternative plan. "I think it is Ceres," she said. "It is the biggest little planet in our solar system. Named after a Greek goddess; Goddess of harvest. What else can it be? I mean, that seems like a reasonable spot where your father could think of hiding the probe."

After doing some additional research, Pete felt Mila might have come up with the answer that potentially fit the riddle, considering all circumstances. Mother was used to address a Goddess. Good grains, love and success all depended on good harvest. In this case - Ceres. The gift could be the probe. If launched from Mars, it wasn't difficult to send something to Ceres. It wasn't too close to Mars, but wasn't that far either. He still needed to find out its exact location but he didn't think it would be too far to travel. He didn't want to take the tourists along, and after discussions with Michele and Jason, decided to wait little longer for the spaceship Gary sent to pick them up. He planned to send Mila and Rico back to Mars as well. There was no need to put them at risk.

# Chapter 22

According to Pete's calculation, it would take them eight to nine days to reach Ceres. Dark Wolf probably could go about three fourth as fast as Space Tiger at best, he assumed. That meant they could still catch up with Wolf. He was ahead by about two days. But Wolf knew this area better. If they miscalculated even by a tiny amount, they might miss the little planet. In that case, speed won't help them much. Pete knew he had no room for mistakes. He needed the best possible solar map of the Sun and its celestial bodies. That was an easy thing to get. He called their controller and requested a complete map, including the orbital map of Ceres. He received it in ten minutes.

In the asteroid belt between Mars and Jupiter, Ceres was the largest celestial body with a diameter at the equator almost 1000 kilometers (600 miles). Gravity was only about three hundredth of what was observed on Earth. It was much smaller than Earth's moon. Temperature was way below zero but still somewhat bearable at -38 degree Celsius. Due to its inefficiency in reflecting back solar light, it had a lower brightness. Under the rocky skin Ceres was covered in thick ice.

Pete didn't know under exactly what circumstances

his father had sent the probe to Ceres, but he could understand the reasoning behind it. Among all the asteroids there was only a handful where a probe could land and more importantly, could be salvaged from. Did Robert Brown plan to return? Or somebody else was supposed to come and get it? Or was it possible that he never wanted anybody to even know where it was. What was in that probe?

Gary's spaceship reached on time. It was relatively modern and fast. The two tourists had already taken the time to get out of their cabin and become familiar with everybody. After such a miserable experience, they were really anxious to get back to Earth. A large scale celebration was being planned on Earth for their return. Along with them, Pete and the crews of the Space Tiger had also become household names on Earth. There were even rumors spreading about the secret affair between Pete and Michelle. Some of the magazines published juicy articles about a triangle love affair. Pete didn't know whether to laugh or cry. How could the papers publish something so unfounded without any real information? Okay, some of the stuff somehow hit the point, but they had no way to know that. The crews got news feed every day. What were they thinking? Pete felt ashamed, especially before Jason. Who knew what was going on in his mind? The last thing he wanted was to lose respect of his crews and friends.

Once the two tourists left, Pete wasted no time and had the Space Tiger zoom toward Ceres in full speed. Mila refused to return to Mars, so both she and Rico were coming with them too. Pete wasn't very excited about it, but he didn't want to make a big deal out of it either, not after both Mila and Rico had proven to be quite useful, not taking account of the stunt that Mila pulled off with the capsule.

Eight-nine days was a long time. Pete had never gone in a trip this long with such young crews. Most of the time there was not much to do in a spaceship. Keeping that in mind, Pete had loaded his spaceship with all kind of gaming instruments, from video to holographic games. One thing he always lamented was the absence of a full size gravity wheel, which needed to be at least seven hundred and fifty feet in diameter and to rotate twice every minute around its axis to provide a feeling of normal gravitational force. The one that Space Tiger had was only two hundred feet in diameter. Due to the smaller size, the wheel was not rotated two times a minute, as that would make the inhabitants feel nauseous and possibly sick. Pete usually set it up to rotate once a minute around its axis. That provided only a fraction of normal gravity but that wasn't too bad. Combined with other technologies, a gravity wheel of that size provided almost the feeling of natural gravity. Inside the gravity wheel there were gymnasium, sports center, dining room, several additional cabins, and a backup control room. During long trips crews could sleep there. The wheel was usually activated during trips that took longer than three days, to conserve energy.

Once activated, the gravity wheel became the central point of attraction for the trainees. It became hard to keep them in the bridge. They explored to the wheel at every opportunity they got and engaged into playing games. With Mila around, they partnered up and competed vigorously. Most of the time Larisa teamed up with Jing Jing leaving Taz and Mila with no other options but to play together. Pete tried his best to send Mila back to Mars but she simply refused to leave. She declared that she wasn't going anywhere without seeing the end of Wolf. Pete had a long discussion with Gary who sounded more helpless than Pete. At the end, with Mila promising not to even move a finger without his permission and Rico staying back as well to keep an eye on her, Pete agreed.

With the trainees in the wheel, Pete, Michelle, Jason and Rico spent most of the time in the bridge. Pete didn't think this trip was long enough for them to start using the control room inside the wheel. After stories spread through the media about Pete and Michelle, Jason had turned pretty quiet, even more than before. Pete thought of discussing it openly with him and clarifying things up, but he couldn't get himself to go through it. If they brought such things into their discussions who knew where that would end up? Instead, he decided to avoid it totally. He passively encouraged Jason and Michelle to spend more time together while he and Rico got into increasingly involving discussion about Mars, Earth and the ever spreading human civilization.

Days went by rather slowly for Pete... one... two...three... The four young crews had no shortage of activities. They kept themselves pretty busy with games and impromptu parties. Pete did some reading. He spoke to Dan several times. He learned, to his relief, that his mother was safe. She was hiding in her parents' mansion. Nobody knew why. Pete called her up but got no answer. He admitted, in the last few years the distance between him and his mother had increased drastically. He made it a point to reconcile once he returned to Earth after this mission. It was obvious Sicily was quite lonely. She tried to keep herself busy with politics and her family. She did have a big successful family. Her parents and siblings all lived nearby and did everything they could to keep her going. But was that enough to replace a husband and a son?

Michelle and Jason held on for three days before joining the youngsters in the games room, with Pete's approval, of course. They quickly became the third team. Pete was happy to see his crew trying to make the best out of the situation. There was really nothing going on in the bridge. In case of an emergency, he could have everybody gather in thirty seconds. But such emergencies seldom occurred. There were very little chances of danger in deep space. Among two of the most probable risks were: they could hit a floating object or get attacked by another ship. Both were rare incidents and weren't something that could happen quietly. The ultra modern monitoring system would caution long ago.

"What do you think? Will we be able to catch Wolf?" Rico asked on day five.

"I have no desire to catch him," Pete chose his words carefully. There was no guarantee that Rico would not inform Gary about things that he felt important. "That is not my responsibility. However, it is important for me to know what is in that probe."

"What if Wolf reaches there first and flies away with the probe?" Rico asked.

"I don't plan to keep chasing him around all over the space. I'll return to Earth. I have trainees with me. I can't pull them into any more risks than I already have. If the company decides to go after Wolf, I might return with a more experienced crew."

"I wish I could work with you. It's not always as much fun living in the City of Mars. After all, it's a small place."

"Even a Smartman can get bored!" Pete laughed.

Rico laughed too. "Why won't he? Don't forget, we have practically all the feelings that a human does. It's just that we don't always express them the same way."

"What do you think about death?" Pete abruptly asked.

"Nothing. We simply don't have the ability to believe in religion, life after death, hell, heaven – all those stuff. We are very materialistic. So, for us dying means going to sleep forever."

"Would you miss your life?"

"I probably will, a little. I'll probably miss the crazy girl," Rico said shyly.

"Can you start a family? I heard Smartmans of latest models do share such feelings of family bondage."

"Not us. Some recent models do have that ability but they tend to be weaker in other areas, especially in cognitive matters."

"Do you ever wish you had a family or the feelings? You know what I mean. What you feel for Mila is probably what a father feels for his daughter."

"I don't really know," Rico said. "It would definitely make things complicated. I guess I am just okay the way I am. What is the use? Why make our life more complex than it is."

"Doesn't look like you are fully immune to so called humanly feelings," Pete smiled.

Rico Shrugged. "I don't know why that's happening."

Eventually eight days passed by. Ceres had become brighter and brighter until it was clearly visible. At one point, the monitor showed it would take them another four hours to reach Ceres. Pete had been diligently working on to find out if Dark Wolf was around. Unfortunately, Space Tiger's radars were unable to pick up any sign of Dark Wolf. That didn't mean it wasn't in the area. There were all kinds of technology available for signal scrambling. Dark Wolf could be using something like that, which would essentially make it invisible to any radar. Space Tiger used a combination of several technologies to avoid being detected as well.

Pete called everybody in the bridge to brief. His plan was to land on Ceres. One thing he knew, Wolf wouldn't leave without the probe. The question was – did he have enough time to salvage the probe and run away with it? Pete had flown Space Tiger at its highest speed. He really doubted that Wolf had made it to Ceres too long ago. According to his calculation, Dark Wolf had to be somewhere nearby.

As they randomly flew around Ceres, it didn't take them too long to find Dark Wolf, sitting on a flat land. A group of Smartmans was operating a machine to pull something out of the ground. Pete circled the area several times keeping good distance. He didn't have to wait very long to get Wolf react.

"You found the answer to the riddle, I guess?" Wolf's voice echoed in the speaker system of the bridge.

"Apparently. Why are you digging earth?" Pete asked, trying to sound nothing more than curious.

"The probe went through the rocky sheet and plunged into the ice after the collision," Wolf said in a matter of fact tone. "It would be better if you didn't come here," he added, after a moment's pause.

"I must know what is in that probe," Pete said. "If you allow me to see it, things could resolve peacefully."

Wolf burst into laughter. "There is nothing called *peaceful* in this universe. I can't let you see the content of that probe. My order is to terminate anybody who comes near it. I was hoping remaining of this trip would go peacefully. But you are really stubborn. You leave me with no other choice but to fight you."

"Do you think you have a winning chance against Space Tiger?" Pete sounded over confident, trying to put doubts in Wolf's mind. "How can that old sheet of metal stand against my ultra modern spaceship?"

"Too cocky, huh!" Wolf chuckled. "Doesn't really fit

you. Don't underestimate my old sheet of metal. It may look like that, but it can go neck to neck with most so called modern spaceships. Anyway, the question is, do you really want to fight? Are you in a position to take the risk of having your trainees getting hurt? Oh, how about Gary's daughter? She must be there too."

Pete smiled to himself. Wolf was nobody's fool. He knew the game, probably much better than Pete did. The crew was staring at him, must be wondering what he was going to say next. "You got me. How about we resolve this without a battle?"

"There is no way to resolve this, Mr. Pete," Wolf said, with a touch of sarcasm. "Either you leave or you fight. The probe is mine. You have no right to it."

"I could care less about the probe," Pete said, thinking fast. "It is yours. Just let me see the content."

Wolf burst into laughter once again. "Why are you being so stubborn? You can't see it. Go away. I let you go once. I cannot afford to do that again. Don't forget, even a bad guy has a boss."

"Who is your boss?"

Wolf laughed lazily. "Did you really expect an answer?"

"Worth a try. Anyway, we are going to land. Don't try anything foolish. My cannons are aimed at your ship. If it gets hit by six full powered laser beams, I doubt it would ever fly again."

"My cannons are also trained on you. I modified the laser beams. One good hit can do a lot of damage to your *modern ship*. Are you sure you want to take that risk?"

He was right again. Space Tiger had a very good defense system, but there was no way to know how well it would hold up against a strong attack. "How about we do this like man?"

"You want to fight me?" Wolf was silent for few moments. "Nobody can call me a coward. This time we'll do this like the middle ages – with swords. You lose you leave. Deal?"

"And what if I win?" Pete asked.

"The probe is yours. I'll disappear," Wolf said.

Michelle muted the microphone. "Your shoulder hasn't fully healed yet. Do you think you can beat him in a sword fight? Why are you being so reckless?"

"It is better than putting all of you at risk," Pete said. "On the other hand, win or lose, Wolf would never leave without the probe. He is just buying some time. If we start an all out battle now, the probe might get destroyed. He just wants to load it into his ship and race out of here. This is what I am planning. When I am fighting Wolf, you'll be trying to snatch that probe away from those Smartmans.

With Wolf distracted, I doubt they would be as effective. Rico, what do you say?"

"It might work," Rico thoughtfully said.

"Come down!" Wolf sounded impatient. "Hopefully, I won't have to fight you ever again."

"Will you be able to hold him off for long enough?" Michelle asked, clearly worried.

"I'll," Pete said, confidently. "I am much younger than him. He won't be able to match my speed. I'll just have to make sure that he can't use laser guns."

"What if he doesn't keep his word? What if he uses a gun? You should keep a gun too," Michelle insisted.

Pete chuckled. "Don't be so worried. I always keep a backup gun inside my shoes. So, if he changes his style, I'll be able to match him too. But you should still keep an eye. If his robot army joins him, I'll need help."

Pete carefully landed the ship on the ground, keeping almost a kilometer distance from the Dark Wolf, with the cannons trained on it. Wolf climbed down his ship, in his all familiar mask. The temperature outside was negative thirty eight degree Celsius. Winter clothing was essential. Wolf had a thick leather trouser and a heavy winter jacket on. The gravity here was only three hundredth of Earth. That essentially meant with every sudden move, no matter how small, they could be thrown up thirty forty feet or more.

Before stepping out to the ground, Pete discussed the overall plan with his team for one last time. While he was determined to find out what was inside that mysterious probe, the last thing he wanted was to put his crews in the mouth of danger without taking proper precautions. He had everybody put on their special suits with extra anti-laser shields at the top of it. The plan was relatively simple. Pete would keep Wolf distracted, while Rico and Jason would attempt to snatch the probe away from Wolf's robots. Michelle would stay back in the ship acting as the controller for the whole operation. She would have Taz as her pilot. Mila, Larisa and Jing Jing would stay inside the ship. If for any reason things didn't work out, it would be Michelle's responsibility to take the remaining crews to safety. Pete specifically instructed her not to engage in any kind of battle with Dark Wolf. Dan would later decide how to handle the situation."

Pete exited through the main gate, slowly and confidently, making sure to have a good entry in the fight. The idea was to create a smokescreen, which would allow Rico and Jason to secretly get off the ship via the cargo door at the back. Pete hopped for several hundred feet and stood facing Wolf keeping a safe distance of about fifty feet. Wolf laughed. "This is going to be lot of fun! We are going to fight like Superman. Ha… ha… ha…"

"You definitely are in good spirit," Pete taunted. "I guess you are really happy about finding the probe. I am just dying to know what is in it."

"I cannot share that with you, unfortunately," Wolf lightly said, matching Pete's sarcasm.

"You have been looking for it for so long! It must have something very valuable," Pete pressed on.

"There may be some truth in that. However, it would be better if you kept out of my business."

"My father had something to do with it. It is now my business. If nothing else, I must know the truth in his honor."

"Well, truth is not always very enlightening. Let's just keep that aside and fight," Wolf said. He was carrying two long, heavy swords. He threw one at Pete. "My favorite weapon. I don't like lasers or bullets. You want to fight, you gotta get dirty."

The sword flew slowly in the air before dropping in front of Pete. He picked it up. It felt so light! Very low gravity made things weigh much less than what they would have weighed back on Earth. Pete himself felt like a paper plane, a slight push could throw him far high into the air. Ceres had some air but not good for breathing.

Wolf looked quite funny as he jumped his way to Pete, uncontrollably, attempting to launch an attack. Pete had considerable amount of training in free hand combat in low gravity environment. One thing he knew very well – trying to do anything abruptly could have disastrous outcome. The good part was, because everything moved so slowly, there was always more time to react. He didn't even move from his place until Wolf came pretty close to him, brandishing his sword in the air, crazily. Pete moved away at the last moment, trying to use as little force as possible. He knew the harder he would press on the ground the further up he would go, messing up his body control.

Wolf learned quickly. After a few failed attacks he figured out the technique and instead of rushing, came ahead in tiny steps, almost rubbing his feet on the ground. For the next several minutes they went on to attack and counter attack, almost comically. Wolf seemed to enjoy the whole experience. At one point he stopped offering to take a break. "I must tell you one thing Pete," he said in a tone that could almost qualify as friendly. "When I left Earth, I also left behind my only son. He was little. I had no choice. I had never contacted them considering their safety. Today, he must be as big as you are. Sometimes I really miss him."

This sudden show of compassion caught Pete a little surprised. A man with a mask, big and bold, talking about his little son, felt very strange. Who would have thought even this man could be sad deep inside?

"What would have happened if you contacted?" Pete tried to keep Wolf busy. Rico and Jason had come down through the cargo door and were now hopping toward the working Smartmans, who had pulled the probe above the ground by now. Wolf, with his back at them, was more nostalgic than alert.

"That is the problem of living a risky life," he said. "My family could be harmed because of my work. I just didn't want to risk that."

"Who are those people playing God with your life? Why are you allowing it? We can help you," Pete tried to sound as authentic as possible.

Wolf laughed lazily. "I chose my way. I must compensate for that with my life. I can't tell you everything, even if I want to. I can't let anything happen to my family." He paused for a moment. "Okay, that's too much talk. Let's get back into fighting."

This time he somersaulted in the air and came rushing relatively fast. Trying to move out of his reach quickly, Pete was flown away more than two hundred feet. Wolf chased him. They fought with the swords for a bit before stopping again, keeping a safe distance. This was a strange environment for a combat – both agreed. Their own hands and legs felt so light that it was hard to believe hitting anybody with those could cause any pain at all. Pete's main goal was to keep Wolf's attention away from the probe. He assumed Wolf's robot army wouldn't be as efficient without him. However, one thing Pete couldn't be sure, if they were keeping Wolf up-to-date through internal radios, tiny electronics that could be planted inside human body. Wolf seemed to be very calculative and Pete wondered if he would be able to fool him. Nevertheless, he decided to move on with his plan.

"What is the name of your son?" Pete asked.

"Lion. Black hair, brown eyes," Wolf said, proudly.

"Is that why you let me go? Do I remind you of your son?" Pete asked.

"I wouldn't say so. Business is business. It had nothing to do with my feelings. You are a dangerous man. Trying to harm you could have some devastating consequences. I didn't want to take any risk."

Pete grinned. He was starting to like this weird man. There was a part in Wolf that went beyond that bad guy image.

# Chapter 23

Rico and Jason did their best to get close to the probe as quietly as possible, but they couldn't go too far. The five Smartmans who were working on the probe hadn't noticed them, but several others who stayed inside the spaceship detected them and almost instantly rushed out to encounter.

Rico counted – six. He gasped. Who knew how many more Smartmans Wolf had in the spaceship? These were relatively advanced models. Not everybody would understand the classification of Smartmans but experienced eyes could figure it out easily. Looking at their movement and design, he knew they could be formidable opponents. Jason was strong but still just a boy. He (Rico) couldn't depend too much on him. Mila could be very useful but she was inside the ship. On the other hand, he didn't really want to pull her into this dangerous situation. Pete was pretty busy with Wolf. There was no chance of getting any help from him. The only strategy seemed to be attack fast and furiously. He decided in a split second, pushed Jason on the ground, got his laser gun out and before the robots had a chance to react, destroyed two of them.

Jason saw Rico shoot in succession and then dive on the ground. He realized Rico went for a quick attack. It worked partially, but there were still four Smartmans standing, who had just started to shoot. Jason got his gun out and shot back several times hitting one of the robots. The remaining three robots marched forward fearlessly with their guns pointed at them, raining down lasers. Sensing imminent danger, they got up and jumped as far away as they could, looking for some kind of shelter to avoid the lasers. The three Smartmans had cleverly spread out, making it very difficult to target them. The group of workers who had pulled the probe out of ice and were now carrying it to Dark Wolf saw them. They left two robots to guard the probe and rest joined the fight with their guns blazing.

"Now we are in real trouble," Rico said. "Two of us can never beat five of them, not when they are fully ready. Forget about getting anywhere near the probe."

"Should I contact Space Tiger?" Jason asked. "Michelle may be able to help us."

"We are too far from the ship. Only the cannons can reach this far. And we don't want cannons. They can destroy the probe."

"What should we do now?" Jason said frantically. The robots were quickly closing on to them.

Before Rico could answer, the main gate opened and jumped out of the Space Tiger Mila with two blazing guns followed by Larisa and Jing Jing. Rico wasn't happy. He didn't want them to get hurt. Mila had special training in close combat and had a powerful laser gun, but there was only one problem – she had a strong tendency toward being reckless. There was no way to say what she might end up doing. The trainees didn't have proper guns and combat training. They shouldn't have come out of the spaceship.

Mila didn't wait for Rico's command. She asked Larisa and Jing Jing to spread out and attacked the robots with all might. This all out attack helped Rico slightly as two more robots went out of action. But they had little time to rejoice as a new team of five robots streamed out of the spaceship.

"The idiot probably has a whole robot factory in there," Rico cried out in desperation.

"What a loser!" Mila bitterly said. "We'll destroy all of them."

"She thinks she is indestructible," Rico said to Jason. "I fear for her. What about Larisa and Jing Jing? Do they know anything about fighting?"

"A little," Jason said. "But we can't depend on them. They don't have good guns either."

"I know!" Rico said as he continued to shift places and shoot. "Why would Michelle allow them to get out?"

Jing Jing and Larisa dived on the ground and stayed low.

Rico and Jason changed directions and went close to the two trainees. "What are you doing here?" Rico bitterly asked.

"We came to help you guys," Larisa said. "Seemed like you could use some help."

"Sure. This is perfect help. Just stay low," Rico said. "If possible, return to the ship."

"No way," Larisa protested. She shot a few times at a robot but her weak laser did little harm.

"How can anybody fight with these worthless guns?" Jing Jing said resentfully.

"Tell me about it," Rico muttered in discontent.


Michelle was observing the situation carefully from the bridge. Once she saw another set of five robots coming out of Dark Wolf, she knew she would have to do something quickly. Rico and company had no chance against so many heavily armed Smartmans. Somebody could get seriously hurt. She checked for Pete. He was busy fighting Wolf. She could see them jumping in the air every few moments and trying to hit each other with the nasty looking swords. She could connect with Pete using remote access but decided against it, fearing it could break his focus and put him into danger. "Taz, will you be able to get the Space Tiger on the air?" She turned to the youngster.

"Yes," Taz confidently said.

"Then fly it to the other side of Dark Wolf. Don't land. There is only one way to stop Wolf. We'll have to target his probe. It is quite risky but we have no choice. They need help."

Taz had immense admiration for Michelle. He did not want to fail her. He remained calm and focused, revisiting the routine of such take offs in his mind several times. Not only had he flown other spaceships, he actually understood the mechanism of taking off. Release the parking gears; engage the engine; setup an initial force; setup an initial height; ensure all related mechanisms are functioning; pull the take off liver to a certain position; unless there is a mechanical problem let the autopilot do the rest. In less than thirty seconds the Space Tiger went off the ground and stopped at a height of about two hundred feet. Taz made it to float like a kite over Dark Wolf. Michelle set one of the cannons dead on the probe. The two robots who were guarding the probe looked surprised. They took no chances and quickly ran away.

"Wolf! Wolf!" Michele's voice burst into a powerful microphone. "We need to talk. Now!"

As soon as Jason saw the Space Tiger taking off, he knew things were about to turn ugly. Looking at Michelle it was difficult to realize how tough she could be, if the situation warranted. He wondered what she was planning this time. If he wasn't so engaged fighting back the robots, he would have connected and get some details from her.

"What is she trying to do," Rico asked with his face tucked in the ground.

"I won't be surprised if she burns Dark Wolf," Jason said.

"That's what she should be doing," Mila cheered. "I would have done the same. If we can destroy the ship, Wolf the idiot would rot here."

Pete had two different goals as he continued to fight Wolf. In one hand he wanted to keep him distracted; on the other hand he wanted to keep the conversation going just in case something valuable came out of Wolf's mouth. One thing he had already figured out - Wolf had a small part in a big conspiracy. He struggled to find out what part Wolf exactly played. Unfortunately, all his attempts to start a meaningful conversation went nowhere. Wolf was one hell of a shrewd man. The only thing he spoke about was his son who he hadn't seen for a long time. He wouldn't even share where on Earth he came from or what his real name was. They continued to fight, but none of them broke any sweat.

It was Wolf who first noticed the Space Tiger taking

off. Pete saw the puzzled look into his face and instantly knew something unexpected was in progress. He looked up, in the same direction as Wolf, and saw the Space Tiger floating up steadily, and the first thought that crossed his mind was – Michele was out of her mind. Where did she think she was going leaving most of her crews out on the ground?

He didn't have to wait too long to find out the answer. He saw the Space Tiger taking position above the Dark Wolf. At this point her plans became crystal clear. Wolf didn't wait. He bolted toward his spaceship. Pete followed him. They went past several hundred yards, hopping. By the time they reached Dark Wolf, the battle had ceased. Wolf's robots had hidden inside the ship. Rico, Jason, Mila, Larisa and Jing Jing had moved away quite far and stayed very low to the ground.

"Wolf! Open the probe!" Michelle's voice burst into the microphone. "I want to see what's inside it."

"No!" Wolf shook his head as he shouted. Michelle had no way to hear him.

"I am not going to repeat myself," Michelle said coldly. "I am giving you ten seconds. If you don't open it up, I'll burn it into ashes."

Pete stopped about forty feet away from Wolf. "She is going to do it," He warned Wolf. Would she? Pete paused think. Hopefully not. He really wanted to know what was in that probe. It could be the key to a very big thing. He prayed that Michelle would not at any circumstance use the cannons on the probe. Having it destroyed would be devastating.

Wolf thought for a few seconds. He shrugged and walked toward the probe. Pete thought Wolf was probably trying to buy some time. He had no intention to do what Michelle asked for. Perhaps he was trying to connect with his Smartmans inside the Dark Wolf and concoct a quick counter attack. Pete continued to follow him keeping a short distance between them. Nobody noticed Mila had moved out of her position and was quickly crawling toward them.

The probe was relatively smaller in size. Twenty years ago these things were made that way. As it was tucked into ice, it had a sheet of ice over it but otherwise looked perfectly intact. A bullet shaped object with several wheels that could even fly on its own, it was about ten feet in length and eight feet in diameter and had only one entrance. Wolf grabbed the sturdy handle and gave it a few good jerks. After a few stubborn moments the door gave up and opened with a bang. Pete could feel his heartbeat going off the roof. What was about to be revealed?

Wolf stood foolishly in front of the open gate as if he had just forgotten how to speak. There was nothing inside the probe, nothing at all! It was completely empty. All that for this!

He entered the probe and checked fruitlessly. When he finally walked out after a few long moments, he had an expression on his face that was in between surprise and confusion. He looked around in a way as if he expected to see other probes lying around, one of which would definitely be the right one.

Pete was about to say something but right at that instance, Mila sprung of the ground and charged at Wolf with her guns blazing. Any other time Wolf would have definitely detected her in time to counter attack or defend himself, but this time his mind was probably little numb from the big surprise. At least four laser shots broke through his laser guard and entered his body. The laser guard worked very well against weaker lasers, but was not that effective against the strong ones. For several moments Wolf looked at his wounds with total bewilderment. Mila continued to advance with her guns raining down lasers on Wolf. Before Wolf's robots stepped in to attack her back, Rico rushed in, grabbed her, pulled her away, and dived to safety.

Wolf ignored the wounds and allowed Rico and Mila to move away. He looked at Pete still displaying pure surprise. "I can't believe this. Where did all the stuff go?"

"What was in there?" Pete stepped forward a few steps, weary of the robots. Would they attack?

He didn't have to wait too long. Before Wolf could respond, half a dozen Smartmans burst out of the Dark Wolf. Each carried heavy laser guns, ready to start a hell. Pete noticed one of the cannons in the Dark Wolf moved and was now pointing at the Space Tiger. Moments later the cannon shot a series of wide laser beams right at the Space Tiger. To his relief, Taz acted promptly and deployed the laser shield that blocked off the beams. The cannons that were aimed at the probe quickly changed direction and were trained on the Dark Wolf. Blood red laser beams zoomed in and bombarded the Dark Wolf, blowing off part of the bridge. The robots behind the control held on and counter attacked with more laser beams of their own. Taz skillfully maneuvered the spaceship to keep it out of harm's way.

Pete realized if they stood there all of them would turn into vapor at some point in near future. He shouted at Rico to go back further, held Wolf with one arm and jumped as far away as he possibly could from the battle zone. Wolf was becoming weak. A wound right under his throat spewed out warm blood. Even if he got good treatment, he probably wouldn't have made it, Pete thought. If he could somehow take him in the Space Tiger he could have tried to stop the bleeding. But at that moment it was an impossible thought. Wolf's men were fighting vigorously showing no intention to surrender regardless of the fact that their captain was seriously injured. Pete was hoping at some point they would figure out that they couldn't win this battle without their leader Wolf and would simply give up. But in reality things happened quite differently. It was possible that Wolf had a set of instructions implanted into his robots to ensure they knew what to do in case something happened to him. The Dark Wolf had received a few good hit from the Space Tiger and was bellowing smoke from various sections. Through that heavy sheet of smoke marched out an army of at least a dozen robot soldiers, who came right at Pete. They were coming to rescue Wolf, Pete reckoned.

Wolf hadn't lost his consciousness yet. His eyes were now murky but he could still hear. "Please stop your Smartmans," Pete urged. "We have nothing against them. I don't want them to get hurt."

Wolf nodded silently. He raised a hand in the air and signaled something. The robot army stopped but held onto their arms, ready to act if needed. Pete connected with Jason and instructed him not to attack them. From the partly destroyed smoke filled spaceship, somebody was still throwing laser bombs at the Space Tiger. As a result, Michelle continued to counter attack. Finally, making everybody's fear a reality, a stray laser beam hit the fuel tank of Dark Wolf. The spaceship burst into flames with tremendous force and bright flashes with heat waves zooming past them. Pete held Wolf and jumped on the ground. His robot army was swept away to oblivion in a blink of eye.

Michelle saw the blast and instructed Taz to move out of the vicinity. Once things settled down a bit she had it landed, keeping a good distance from the burning spaceship. Two of them carefully climbed down.

Wolf was lying down on the ground on his back. A pool of blood was collecting around him. Pete sat on his knees beside him. He wanted to hold his head high but Wolf asked him not to. He was a proud, egoistic man. Pete looked around. Rico, Mila, Jason, Larisa and Jing Jing were now up on their feet. They teamed up and advanced toward him and Wolf cautiously.

Pete checked on Wolf. He wasn't going to make it. Rico and the rest were still several hundred feet away. He hated to do this to a dying man but he had no choice. "Wolf, tell me one thing," Pete almost whispered to Wolf. "What was my father's role into all this?"

Wolf looked at him with foggy eyes. "Don't worry. Your father did not do anything wrong."

"What was in that probe?"

Wolf tried to sigh. A spit of blood came out of his mouth. He probably thought for a few moments whether to answer or not. "Treasure," he finally said.

"Treasure!"

Wolf's eyes were closed. His breathing had stopped. Pete tried to feel his pulse. Nothing. Wolf had died. Who knew why, but Pete felt a little bad. Perhaps he thought about Lion. The strange man had surely made some sort of weird connection with Pete. Did Wolf want him to find Lion? Or why else would he mention his son to him? Could Lion be in danger? He promised to himself to find Lion when he goes back to Earth.

Michelle and Taz joined the rest and walked to Pete.

"Are you okay?" Michelle asked softly.

"Yes. Any injuries?" He looked at everybody to visually inquire.

Mila looked at the dead body with a twist in her lips. Her hands went up to her waists. "Thanks God! The pest is gone. I am so happy."

Rico didn't look very happy. "Did you find out what is in the probe?" he asked. "Not this empty one. The one he was expecting."

Pete nodded. "Yes".

"Really!" They exclaimed in sync. "What is it?"

"Treasure!" Pete said. "That's exactly what he said. Who knows what he was referring to? Anyway, we got to get back into the ship."

Pete started to walk toward Space Tiger with the rest

following him closely.

# Chapter 24

After dropping Rico and Mila in Mars, Pete returned to Earth with his crew. Taz had expected Mila would give him her phone number or something of that nature to keep in touch. If he was a little less shy he might have just asked for it. Mila didn't offer anything and just waved when they left Mars. Taz felt really bad. He beat himself up for not having the courage to ask. During their travel back to Earth, Larisa teased him relentlessly for that. He tried to make light of it but apparently nobody was buying any of it and they all just knew how much he was in love with a Martian girl – quite exotic and ridiculously reckless.

After returning to Earth, Pete had taken them to a very good restaurant. This was an exception. Due to security reasons, when they were not in a mission, they weren't supposed to contact each other unless required. Dan had joined them in the dinner too. With his big stature he ate like an elephant and had everybody rolling their eyes. Pete tried to give him lectures about his overweight and overeating but he did not pay attention to that. Even CI-6 called in to inquire what they had ordered. Unfortunately, to him, none of it made any difference. He even mockingly cried about that for a little bit. He really wanted to be able to eat.

Before they left, everybody had a simple question to Dan and Pete. Were they going in another mission any time soon? They would love to go back to Mars. There were so much to see and they had so little time to explore. Dan just smiled and did not say anything. Pete shrugged mysteriously as if to say - *Who knew? Anything was possible.*

Since he returned home, Taz had to spend days to assuage the overwhelming curiosity of his family. But he had cautioned all of them a million times, not to share any of it with anybody else outside the family. There could be serious consequences. Uncle Alam had visited several times to get all the details. Taz had suddenly become an important person in the family. But he had fallen back in his studies at school. He tried to forget everything about the trip and focused on to catching up with his studies.

After couple of weeks a tiny email came from Mars.

"Write me. – Mila."

www.ingramcontent.com/pod-product-compliance
Lightning Source LLC
Chambersburg PA
CBHW060530180626
46817CB00002B/503